"If you have this under control, I should go."

Madeline glanced at her watch. "I have to be at work in an hour."

Jackson nodded, distracted. Even distracted he could make a woman take a second look. His suntanned face was angular but strong. Fine lines crinkled at the corners of his eyes. His mouth, which often turned in an easy, *gotcha* smile, was now held in a serious line.

"Could you stay, just until I figure this out?" Jackson's words stopped her as she started to turn away. "Please."

Softer, a little more pleading.

Reluctant, Madeline looked at the cowboy leaning against the door as if he needed it to hold him up.

He cleared his throat. She looked up, met his humor-filled gaze and managed a smile.

"I think it would be better if you called your family, Jackson."

There, she'd been strong. She could walk away. He had people to help him.

But she couldn't walk away. Not from the teen girl dropped on his doorstep. Certainly not from the cowboy standing in front of her.

Books by Brenda Minton

Love Inspired

Trusting Him
His Little Cowgirl
A Cowboy's Heart
The Cowboy Next Door
Rekindled Hearts
Blessings of the Season
  "The Christmas Letter"
Jenna's Cowboy Hero
The Cowboy's Courtship
The Cowboy's Sweetheart
Thanksgiving Groom
The Cowboy's Family
The Cowboy's Homecoming
Christmas Gifts
  "Her Christmas Cowboy"
The Cowboy's Holiday Blessing

BRENDA MINTON

started creating stories to entertain herself during hour-long rides on the school bus. In high school she wrote romance novels to entertain her friends. The dream grew and so did her aspirations to become an author. She started with notebooks, handwritten manuscripts and characters that refused to go away until their stories were told. Eventually she put away the pen and paper and got down to business with the computer. The journey took a few years, with some encouragement and rejection along the way—as well as a lot of stubbornness on her part. In 2006 her dream to write for Love Inspired came true. Brenda lives in the rural Ozarks with her husband, three kids and an abundance of cats and dogs. She enjoys a chaotic life that she wouldn't trade for anything—except, on occasion, a beach house in Texas. You can stop by and visit at her website, www.brendaminton.net.

The Cowboy's Holiday Blessing

Brenda Minton

Love Inspired

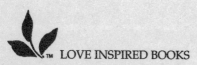

Recycling programs
for this product may
not exist in your area.

LOVE INSPIRED BOOKS

ISBN-13: 978-0-373-87712-6

THE COWBOY'S HOLIDAY BLESSING

Copyright © 2011 by Brenda Minton

Printed in U.S.A.

Come to me, all you who are weary and burdened,
and I will give you rest.
—*Matthew* 11:28

Merry Christmas to all of you,
and a special thank-you to Stephanie Newton,
Nancy Ragain, Barbara Warren and
Shirlee McCoy, great friends who helped me
so much during the writing of this book.

To Bonnie, Ed and Willie,
for helping to carry the load at church.

To Mary, for a clean house.

To my family, for always putting up with me
during the deadline crunch.

To my editor, Melissa Endlich,
for encouragement at just the right moment.

Chapter One

The rapid-fire knock on the door shook the glass in the living room window. Jackson Cooper covered his face with the pillow he jerked out from under his head, and then tossed the thing because it smelled like the stinking dog that was now curled at his feet, taking up too much room on the couch.

The person at the front door found the doorbell. The chimes sounded through the house and the dog growled low, resting his head on Jackson's leg. The way his luck went, it was probably one of his siblings coming to check on him. This could go two ways. Either they'd give up, knowing he was alive and ignoring them, or they'd break the door down because they assumed the worst.

He opted for remaining quiet and taking his chances. Moving seemed pretty overrated at the moment. Three nights of sleeping on the couch after a horse decided to throw him into the wall of the arena, and this morning it felt like a truck had run over him.

The way he figured it, after another attempt or two they'd give up. Unless the "they" in question weren't his siblings, but instead someone with literature and an invitation to church. Or it could be that girl he dated last month, the one that wouldn't stop calling. He covered his face with his arm and groaned. The dog at his feet sat up.

The door rattled again and the dog barked. The next time they knocked harder. Jackson shot the dog a look and Bud cowered a little.

"Thanks, you mangy mutt."

He sat up, careful to breathe deep. Bruised kidneys, cracked ribs and a pulled muscle or two. Man, he was getting too old for this. He'd given up bull riding a few years back for the easier task of raising bulls and training horses. Every now and then a horse got the best of him, though.

He got to his feet and headed for the door, moving slowly and taking it easy. He buttoned his shirt as he walked. The dog ran ahead of him and sat down in front of the door.

When he got to the door he looked in the mirror on the wall and brushed his hands through his shaggy hair. He rubbed a palm across whiskers that should have seen a razor days ago.

"I'm coming already." He jerked the door open and the two people on his front porch stared like they'd just seen a man from Mars.

He glanced down. Yeah, his jeans were the same ones he'd worn yesterday and his shirt was pretty threadbare, but he was fully clothed and decent. He ran a hand through his hair again and tried to smooth it down a little.

"What?" If they were selling cookies or raffle tickets, he wasn't going to be happy. Take that back; he already wasn't happy.

The woman frowned and he remembered her. She'd

moved into the old homestead a year or so back. She wore her typical long sweater, longer skirt and her hair in a ponytail. The glasses that framed big, brown eyes were sliding down her nose. He shook his head and focused on the girl next to her. A kid with blond hair and hazel-green eyes. Man, those eyes looked familiar.

"Mr. Cooper, we... I..." The schoolteacher stumbled over her words. He was on painkillers but he remembered her name: Madeline. Yesterday he'd barely remembered his own name, so that was definitely an improvement.

He grinned because the more he smiled, the more flustered she always got. At that moment she was pulling her heavy sweater a little tighter. A week or so back he'd helped her put groceries in her car and she'd nearly tripped trying to stay away from him.

"Ms. Patton."

"Mr. Cooper," she said, pushing her glasses back in place. She was cute, in a schoolmarm kind of way. "Mr. Cooper, this young lady was dropped off at my house."

"And this young lady is my problem why?" He shifted his attention from Madeline Patton to the girl at her side.

The girl glared at him. He guessed her to be about thirteen. But for all he knew she was sixteen. Or ten. Kids grew up too fast these days. And yeah, when had he started sounding like his parents? He'd kind of thought if he didn't get married and have kids it wouldn't happen.

Wrongo.

He leaned against the door frame. The dog had joined him and was sitting close to his legs, tongue lapping up cool air.

"Mr. Cooper, it is your problem..."

"Call me Jackson." He grinned and she turned three shades of red. He could do one shade better than that. "And I'll call you Maddie."

Yep, from rose to pure scarlet cheeks.

"Madeline." Her little chin raised a notch as she reminded him. "Please let me finish."

He nodded and kept his mouth shut. Time to stop teasing the teacher. But for the craziest reason, one he couldn't grab hold of at the moment, he couldn't stop smiling at her. Maybe he'd never noticed before that her smile was sweet and her eyes were soft brown.

Maybe it was the pain meds talking to his addled brain, scrambling his thoughts the way his insides were already scrambled. Something was causing random thoughts to keep running through his mind. Worse, to jump from his mouth.

"Mr. Cooper, this young lady was dropped off at my house by her aunt. She left the girl and drove away." She paused a long moment that felt pretty uncomfortable. He got the distinct impression that she was making a point, and he didn't get it.

"Why is that my problem?"

The girl stepped forward. A kid in a stained denim coat a size too small and tennis shoes that were worn and holey. She brushed back blond hair with bare hands red from the cold. When had it gotten this cold? A week ago it had been in the sixties.

The kid gave him a disgusted look. "What she's trying to tell you is that I'm your daughter."

"Excuse me?" He looked at her and then at the teacher. Madeline Patton shrugged slim shoulders.

"I'm your daughter."

He raised his hand to stop her. "Give me a minute, okay?"

Jackson rubbed his hand through his hair and took a deep breath. Deep as he could. He turned his attention back to the girl with the hazel-green eyes. He noticed then that the blond hair was sun-bleached, sandy brown more than blond.

The kid stared back at him, probably waiting for him to say or do something. Now, what in the world was he supposed to do?

"Aren't you going to say something?" She stepped close, a determined look on her face.

"Can you give me a minute? It isn't like I got a chance to prepare for this. It's early and I wasn't sitting around thinking a kid would show up on my door today, claiming to be mine."

"Mr. Cooper—" Madeline Patton stepped forward, a little cautiously "—I know this is awkward but we should probably be calm."

"Calm?" He laughed at the idea of the word. "I didn't plan on having the postal service deliver a package to my house today. I certainly didn't expect a special delivery that walks, talks and claims to be mine."

It really wasn't possible. But he could keep some random thoughts to himself. He could take a deep breath and deal with this.

"Why do you think I'm your dad?"

The girl gave him another disgusted look and then dug around in the old red backpack she pulled off her shoulder. She shoved past some clothing and a bag of makeup. Finally she pulled out a couple of papers and handed them to him.

"Yeah, so I guess you're the clueless type," she said.

Nice. He took the papers and looked at them. One was a birth certificate from Texas. He scanned the paper and nearly choked when he got to the father part—that would be the line where his name was listed. Her mother's name was listed as Gloria Baker. The date, he counted back, was a little over thirteen years ago. Add nine months to that and he could almost pinpoint where he'd been.

Fourteen years ago he'd been nineteen, a little crazy and riding bulls. At that age he'd been wild enough to do just about anything. Those were his running-from-God years. That's what his grandmother called them. His mom had cried and called him rebellious.

He handed the birth certificate back to the kid. Her name was Jade Baker. He wanted a good deep breath but it hurt like crazy to take one. He looked at the second paper, a letter addressed to him. Sweet sentiment from a mom who said Jade was his and he should take care of her now. The handwriting had the large, swirling scrawl of a teenager who still used hearts to dot the *i*.

The name of her mother brought back a landslide of memories, though. He looked at the kid and remembered back, remembered a face, a laugh, and then losing track of her.

"Where's your aunt?"

"Gone back to California. She said to tell you I'm your problem now."

"And Gloria?" Her mother. He kind of choked on the word, the name. He hadn't really known her. Madeline Patton gave him a teacher look.

"She died. She had cancer."

Now what? The kid stood in front of him, hazel eyes filling up with tears. He should do something, call someone, or take her home. Where was home? Did she have other family? He didn't know anything about Gloria Baker.

He looked at Madeline, hoping she had something to say, even a little advice. The only thing she had for him looked to be a good case of loathing. Nice. He'd add her name to the list. It was a long list.

"I'm sorry." He handed the papers back to Jade. "But kid, I'm pretty sure I'm not your dad."

Madeline Patton had pulled the girl into her soft embrace while giving him a look that clearly told him to do something about this situation. What was he supposed to do? Did she expect him to open his door to a teenage girl, welcome her in, buy her a pony?

He had known Gloria Baker briefly years ago. He'd never laid eyes on Jade. He wasn't anyone's dad. He was about the furthest thing from a dad that anyone could get.

This wasn't what he wanted. The kid standing in front of him probably wasn't too thrilled, either.

"We'll have to do something about this." He realized he didn't have a clue. What did a guy do about something like this, about a kid standing on his front porch claiming to be his?

First he had to take control. He pointed into the living room. "Go on in while I talk to Ms. Patton."

Jade hurried past him, probably relieved to get inside where it was warm. Madeline Patton stared over his shoulder, watching the girl hurry inside, the dog following behind her. He didn't know Madeline Patton, other than in passing, but he imagined that momentarily she'd have a few choice things to say to him.

Madeline watched Jade walk into the living room and then she turned her attention back to Jackson Cooper. He remained in the doorway, faded jeans and a button-up shirt, his hair going in all directions. Her heart seemed to be following the same path, but mostly was begging for a quick exit from this situation.

Although she didn't really know Jackson Cooper, she thought she knew him. He was the type of man that believed every woman in the world loved him. Well, maybe this would teach him a lesson.

The thought no more than tumbled through her mind and her conscience took a dig at her. This situation shouldn't be about a lesson learned. A child deserved more than this.

And Jackson Cooper wasn't the worst person in the world. He'd come to her rescue last week when a bag of groceries had broken, spilling canned goods across the parking lot of the store. He'd been fishing and was suntanned and smelled of the outdoors and clean soap and was on his way home, but he'd stopped to gather up her spilled groceries, holding them in his T-shirt as he carried them to her car.

Jade had disappeared into the living room. Time for Madeline to make her exit.

"If you have this under control, I should go." She glanced at her watch. "I have to be at work in an hour."

The wind blew, going straight through her. She pulled her sweater close and stomped her booted feet. Jackson nodded, distracted. Even distracted he could make a woman take a second look.

His suntanned face was angular but strong. Fine lines crinkled at the corners of his eyes, eyes that were nearly the same color as Jade's; a little more gray than green. His mouth, the mouth that often turned in an easy, *gotcha* smile, was now held in a serious line.

"I really need to go." Madeline didn't know what else to say, or how to remove herself from this situation, this moment.

"Could you stay, just until I figure this out?" Jackson's words stopped her as she started to turn away. "Please."

Softer, a little more pleading.

Reluctant, Madeline looked at the cowboy leaning against the door as if he needed it to hold him up. She'd heard the ambulance going down the road the other day when he got hurt. They had prayed for him at her Thursday Bible study.

A smile almost sneaked up on her because his grandmother prayed for him, too. The woman who had sold her little house to Madeline never failed to mention Jackson when prayer requests were made on Sunday mornings at the Dawson Community Church. Sometimes she even included fun little details about his social life. Once or twice Madeline had heard a gasp from various members of the church.

He cleared his throat. She looked up, met his humor-filled gaze and managed a smile.

"I think it would be better if you called your family, Jackson." There, she'd been strong. She could walk away. He had people to help him.

"Right, that sounds like a great idea." He no longer smiled. "If I wanted them all over here in my business, that would be the perfect thing to do."

"They're probably going to find out about her anyway, since she stopped at the Mad Cow and asked for directions. Unfortunately she was one house off."

Madeline couldn't figure out how anyone could confuse her little house on two acres with this house on hundreds of acres. She felt tiny on the long front porch of the vast, white farmhouse that Jackson Cooper had remodeled. His grandparents had built this house after their marriage. But his grandfather had grown up in the little house Madeline bought from his grandmother.

The Coopers had a long history in Dawson, Oklahoma.

Her legacy was teaching at School District Ten, and building a home for herself in Dawson. And this time she planned on staying. She wouldn't run.

"Give us thirty minutes, Madeline." Jackson's voice didn't plead, but he sounded pretty unsure. It was that tone that took her by surprise, unsettled her.

She wondered how it felt to be him and have control stripped away by a thirteen-year-old girl. It was for that girl that she even considered staying.

She hadn't been much older than Jade when she'd found herself in a new home and a new life. She would always remember how her sister had dragged her from bed, leading her through the dark, to safety.

"I'll come in for a moment, but I don't know how that will help."

"Me neither, but I don't think you should leave her here alone."

"She isn't *my*—" Madeline lowered her voice "—problem. I don't know her. She says she's your daughter."

"Right, I get that, but let's assume she isn't and play this safe."

Okay, maybe he wasn't as reckless as she had always imagined.

"So, are you a decent cook?" he asked as he led her into his expansive living room with polished hardwood floors and massive leather furniture. The dog and Jade were sitting on the couch, huddled together.

"I don't have time to cook." Madeline tried hard not

to stare, but the house invited staring. It had the sparseness of a bachelor's home but surprising warmth.

"Just asking, sorry." He smiled at Jade then at her. "So, what are we going to do?"

"Do?" Better yet, "we"? He didn't need to include her in this problem.

"Yeah, do. I mean, we should probably call someone. Family services?"

"That's a decision you'll have to make."

"Right." He pointed for her to sit down.

Madeline sank into the luxurious softness of one of the two brown leather sofas. The one opposite had a blanket and pillow indicating he'd been sleeping there.

No Christmas tree. No decorations.

Jackson stood in the center of the living room. The light that filtered through the curtains caught bits and pieces of his expression as he stared at the young girl sitting on his sofa. They stared at each other and then both glanced away.

Madeline didn't know how to help. She could deal with children in a classroom. This seemed to be more of a family situation. And she had no experience with those.

"Maybe you should sit down?" She didn't know what else to say. It wasn't her home. Jackson stood in the center of the room, hands in his pockets. When she made the suggestion, he nodded once. Jade, sitting next to her, gave a disgusted snort.

Madeline sighed. She glanced around the big room, because the silence was uncomfortable and she wanted to head for the door. She glanced at her watch and then looked around the room again. A big stone fireplace took up the wall at the end of the room. The fire that crackled came from gas logs, not wood. A television hung over the fireplace. The walls were textured and painted a warm, natural color. If it hadn't been for the nervous energy of Jackson Cooper standing there staring at her, and then at the girl claiming to be his daughter, Madeline might have enjoyed being in this room.

Jackson moved a chair from the nearby rolltop desk and straddled it backward. He draped his arms over the back rest and sat there, staring at Jade. His legs were stretched out in front of him. His feet were bare.

Madeline picked up the throw pillow leaning against the arm of the couch and held it in her lap. Next to her, Jade fiddled with her ragged little backpack.

Madeline did not belong in this little drama. She had to come up with something to move the action along so she could escape.

"Why did your aunt leave you here?" Jackson asked, zeroing in on the girl with a question Madeline had asked and not gotten an answer for.

Madeline shifted to look at the girl, who suddenly looked younger than her thirteen years. Jade shrugged and studied the backpack in her arms.

"Well?" Jackson might not have kids, but he had a dozen siblings and some were quite a bit younger. His parents had adopted a half dozen or so children to go along with the six biological Coopers. And then there had been Jeremy.

Next to her, Jade looked up, glaring at the man in front of them. She chewed on her bottom lip, not answering Jackson's question. This wasn't going to get them anywhere.

"Jade, we need to know what is going on. We might need to call the proper authorities." Madeline smiled to herself. The word *authorities* always did the trick. The girl's eyes widened and her mouth opened.

"My aunt can't take care of me. She doesn't have the money or a house for us."

Jackson rubbed the back of his neck and when he looked at Madeline, she didn't know what to say or do. She taught English at the local school. She wasn't a counselor. She no longer had siblings. The other foster children in the home where she'd spent a few years until she turned eighteen hadn't counted.

"Maybe we should have coffee." Madeline glanced at the man sitting across from her.

Jackson smiled that smile of his, the one he probably thought conquered every female heart. With good reason. There probably wasn't a single woman under seventy living in and around Dawson who didn't sigh when Jackson crossed her path. But she wasn't one of the women chasing after him. And she certainly wasn't the type he chased.

"You know, some coffee would be good. Do you have time?"

"I can make coffee, but then I have to go. School is out but it's a teacher work day." She glanced at her watch again, and not at Jackson. "You should call your parents."

Because this had nothing to do with her.

But years ago she'd been a kid like Jade, lost and alone, looking for someone to keep her safe. As much as she wanted to run from this situation, she couldn't leave Jade alone.

Chapter Two

The schoolteacher looked at her watch again and then she sighed. He nearly sighed in unison because he didn't know what to do with the kid sitting across from him. Madeline Patton taught school. She had to know more than him.

Jackson pushed himself up from the chair, groaning a little at the spasm in his back. He held the back of the chair and hoped it didn't roll away, because if it did, he'd be face-first on the floor in front of God and everyone.

Madeline stood, too. She faced him, looking him over as he stood trying to get his balance. His lower back clenched and he managed a smile to cover up the grimace.

"Are you okay?" Madeline faced him, her brown eyes narrowing as she watched him, her gaze settling on his white-knuckled grip on the back of the office chair.

"I'm good…" He was great. "I think I'll make that pot of coffee and try to sort this out."

Some kid had knocked on his door, claiming to be his. He had broken ribs and a messed-up back. He was wonderful. Every day should start this way. He managed a smile because it wasn't Madeline Patton's fault.

"Maybe she should go with you?" he offered, a little bit hopeful that he was right about her being worried.

"No, she shouldn't." Another little glance at her watch.

"I'm in the room." The girl slumped on the couch and Bud had curled up next to her. The dog raised its head and growled at him. Yeah, well, his hackles were raised, too.

Jackson shook his head and turned his attention back to Ms. Patton. "What do I do with her?"

"I'd start with feeding her."

He sat down, hard. The chair rolled a little. "Right, feed her. I think there's more to it than that."

"I know there is." She hefted her huge purse to her shoulder.

Concern flickered through those brown eyes. He hadn't meant to play her. He was long past games. In the words of his niece, *games were so last year.*

Yeah, he was going through a mid-life crisis, but Madeline didn't need to know that. She didn't need to know that he envied Wyatt Johnson for settling down with someone he'd wake up with every morning. Man, he was even jealous of Andie and Ryder Johnson's twin girls.

Jackson had two rocking chairs on the front porch, and at night he sat alone and watched the cattle graze in the field. He was as sick of being alone as a man could get. But most of the women his age, if they were still single, were listening to their biological clocks. They were ready for rings and babies.

Which brought him back to the problem at hand: Jade Baker.

"I'll get the coffee started, then you need to make a plan," Madeline offered.

"Thanks, that would be great." He smiled at her and she didn't even flinch. He was losing his touch or she was immune. Either way, he was a little baffled.

"Where's the kitchen?"

He pointed to the wide doorway that led to the dining room and from there to the kitchen and family room. Madeline nodded and away she went, that long skirt of hers swishing around her legs.

"Why don't you just give me a hundred bucks or something and I'll head on down the road." The kid, Jade, shot the comment at him.

Jackson turned the chair to face her. She was hugging his dog. She looked younger than thirteen, maybe because she looked sad and kind of lost. Wow, that took him back to Mia when she'd landed on their doorstep twenty years ago. Travis, nearly twenty-five years ago. Jesse when he'd been about twelve. Jesse had been an angry kid. Now he was a doctor.

Jade Baker, aka his kid. She'd asked for a hundred bucks to leave. Surely the little thing wasn't working him for money? Could it be she'd been dropped off by someone who knew she resembled their family? He rubbed his thumb across his chin and studied her. She just stared at him, with eyes that looked like his and Reece's. Eyes that looked like Heather's and Dylan's.

He could smell toast in the toaster. Jade glanced toward the door that led to the dining room and the kitchen. The dog perked up, too. The girl had pulled her blond hair into a ponytail. Her jeans were threadbare and her T-shirt was stained. He didn't know a thing about her life or what she'd been through.

He hadn't really known Gloria. She'd been about his

age and she'd liked hanging out at rodeos. Someone had told him she lived in the back of a van with her older sister. He hadn't believed it. He should have. The next time he'd gone through the Texas town where he'd met her, she wasn't there.

Fourteen years ago. He barely remembered her. But seeing Jade, the memories resurfaced. He hadn't loved Gloria. He let out a sigh. A kid should at least have that knowledge, that her parents loved each other.

He stood up, holding his breath to get through the pain.

"Sorry, kid, I'm not giving you money. We'll figure this out, but money isn't going to be part of the deal."

"Why not? You obviously don't want me here. With some money I can hit the road and find a place to live."

He admired her pluck. She had stood, and his stupid dog, Bud, stood next to her. "You're not even fourteen yet. You can't live by yourself or even take off on your own. And one hundred dollars? That wouldn't get you to Tulsa."

"I could get emancipated."

"Honey, at your age you can't spell that word and you can't even get a job. We'll try for plan B, okay? Let's go see what Ms. Patton is cooking up in there." He eased forward a couple of steps. Jade glared at him and started to walk away. He reached for her arm and stopped her.

"Let go of me." She turned, fire sparking in those hazel-green eyes of hers.

"I'll let go, but you're not going to blame me for not knowing about you." He'd made a lot of mistakes that he'd had to own up to. He sure wouldn't have walked out on a kid.

He would have claimed his kid if he'd known about

her. If it was possible that she was his, he'd do everything he could for her. But she wasn't his. He was pretty sure of that.

"Yeah, well, you do kind of have something to do with my life and not being in it," she shot back at him, her chin hiking up a few notches and a spark in those eyes that dared him to tell her otherwise.

"I didn't know where your mother went to, and she never tried to get in touch." He had let go of her arm and they stood in the center of the living room, facing off.

"Yeah, well..." Jade stared at him, her eyes big in a little-girl face. Man, she was a tough kid. He didn't know what to do. He could hug her. Or he could just stand there and stare. He didn't think she'd want either.

"Well, what?"

"Well, you coulda tried." Her bottom lip started to tremble. "Haven't you heard of the internet?"

"If I'd known, I would have searched the whole world to find a kid of mine." He softened his tone and took a step forward.

"Yeah, right. My mom said you told her once that you never planned on having kids and so she didn't bother telling you that you had one."

"That was real nice of her to do that." He wasn't going to say anything against her mother. The kid had gone through enough, and he didn't know Gloria well enough to say much more.

She reached for his hand. "I didn't think you'd be so old."

"Well, thanks, Jade. Is Jade short for something?"

"Just Jade." She had hold of his hand. He looked at her hand in his, small and strong. Yeah, he would have been okay with having her for a kid.

* * *

The toast popped out of the toaster and coffee poured into a cup from the single-cup brewer on his counter. Jackson Cooper had the kitchen of her dreams. It didn't seem fair that he had her coffeemaker, the replica of a vintage stove and fridge she'd always dreamed of, granite countertops and light pine floors. But really, what was fair?

Life? Most often not. She'd learned that at an early age. She'd put away the baggage of her past years ago, when she realized carrying it around weighed a person down. If a person meant to let go of their burdens, they shouldn't pack them back up and heft them over their shoulder.

She pulled toast from the toaster and buttered it. From the dining room she could hear Jackson talking to the teenager who had knocked on her door just over an hour ago. A few minutes later they walked into the kitchen and their likeness floored Madeline. The two had the same strong cheekbones, the same strong mouth, and eyes that matched. Jade's hair was lighter.

Jackson walked to the sink and ran water into a glass. Madeline stood next to the counter, feeling out of place in this mess of his and even more out of place in his home. This wasn't where she'd expected to end up today, in Jackson Cooper's kitchen, in his life. When she woke up this morning, it had been like any other Friday. She'd been looking forward to the weekend and decorating her house for Christmas. Jackson hadn't figured into her plans. Ever.

She'd lived in Dawson for over a year, and even though it was a small town, she didn't run in the same circles as Jackson Cooper. Every now and then he flirted with her at the Mad Cow Café. But Jackson flirted with everyone.

"You made toast." Jackson set the glass down on the counter.

"I did, and the coffee is ready." She dried her hands and watched as he shook two pills into his hand, popped them into his mouth and washed them down with water.

"Are you eating?" He pushed a plate in her direction.

"I had a granola bar." She pushed it back. "You need something in your stomach."

"Right." He glanced at the girl that she'd delivered to his front door. "There's cinnamon and sugar in the cabinet if you want it for your toast. After we eat we'll figure this mess out."

Jade carried her plate to the table and sat down. "I don't know what you need to figure out. Fourteen years ago, you messed up." She shot him a look and flapped her arms like wings. "Your roosters have come home to roost."

"Great, she's a smart-mouth to boot," he grumbled as he picked up a slice of toast.

He took a bite and glanced out the window. He didn't sit down. Instead he stood next to Madeline, his hip against the counter. His arm brushed hers. Of course he would be comfortable in his own skin. He wouldn't feel the need for space.

She stepped away from him, picking up a pan that had been next to the sink. Not her pan. Not her mess. She grabbed a scrubber and turned on hot water. Jackson rinsed his plate and opened the dishwasher.

"You don't have to wash that." He touched her arm.

"I don't mind washing it." She rinsed the pan and stuck it in the dish drainer. She glanced out the window again. The land here rolled gently and was dotted with trees. Cattle grazed and a few horses were chasing each other in a circle, bucking and kicking as wind picked up leaves.

"Can she stay with you?"

"Excuse me?" Madeline glanced in Jade's direction and turned her attention back to Jackson.

"Look, Maddie…"

She lifted a hand to stop him. "My name is Madeline."

"Sure, okay, *Madeline.* I need to work this out and you can't leave a kid here with a single man, not when you aren't sure if that single man is her father. And I don't really want my family to know about this, not yet."

"So you want to hide her at my house?" She tapped her foot on the light pine floor and fought the urge to slug him.

"Not hide her. She needs to stay somewhere and she can't really stay here, not until we know exactly what's going on."

As much as she didn't want to, she got it. She also kind of admired him for thinking about the girl. They could call the police or family services, but then she'd end up in state custody. Jade definitely couldn't stay alone with him, a single man. What if she wasn't his? Even if she was, there were things to consider.

She glanced across the room at Jade and she remembered that first night, fourteen and alone in the Montana town she'd rarely visited as a kid. Frightened because she had fifty dollars and no one to turn to, she remembered flashing lights at a convenience store and being driven to a group home.

Fear knotted in her stomach, the way it had then, half a lifetime ago.

"Yes, she can stay with me for a little while."

Jackson watched her, his eyes narrowing. "You sure?"

"Yes, I'm sure."

"I'll pay you." His mouth shifted into a smile, revealing a dimple in his chin.

"Pay me?"

"For letting her stay with you. I can write you a check or pay you cash."

Madeline glanced at her watch. "I really have to go, and I don't want your money."

"There will be the expense of feeding her. She probably needs clothes. I need to pay you something."

Jade stood, the quick movement catching Madeline's attention, and from the jerk of his head in that direction, Jackson's also. The girl held her plate, trembling a little.

"Stop, okay? I'm a kid, not something you trade off or try to get rid of. I thought it would be different..." Jade bit down on her bottom lip and looked from Madeline to Jackson. "You were supposed to be different."

His smile dissolved. Madeline watched as he approached the girl who might possibly be his daughter. He sat down at the table and pointed for her to sit back down. He was used to girls, used to kids. He had been raised in a house with eleven other children. Now he had nieces and nephews.

"Different than what?" he asked.

"Different, that's all."

"From?"

"From my mom. I thought it would be—" she looked away "—better here."

Jackson whistled. "So far we haven't made much of an impression, huh?"

Madeline wanted to correct him, to tell him *he* hadn't made a good impression. The girl claimed to be his. Madeline was just the unsuspecting stranger who had ended up with Jade on her doorstep. And she'd gotten tangled up in this.

"No, you haven't made a great impression." Jade rubbed her eyes hard. Madeline pulled tissues out of a box on the counter and handed them to her. Jade took them with a watery smile and rubbed her nose and then her eyes.

"Okay, let's start over. Jade, I'm Jackson Cooper and I don't know squat about raising teenage girls. Today one landed on my front porch and I'm trying like crazy to figure out what to do and to keep that from being a problem for both of us." He glanced at Madeline. "And this isn't *her* problem at all."

"I don't like being called a problem," the girl cried again.

"Right, okay, you're not a problem. But you are a situation that I need to figure out. And I need a little time to do that."

"Okay."

"So for now, you'll go with Ms. Patton because that's the best thing for us to do. And I'll work at figuring something out."

"She can't go with me yet," Madeline interrupted. "I have to be at work. Now!"

"Okay, so we'll work this out. She stays with me for now while you go to work and later we figure something out."

"Jade, I'll see you later." Madeline leaned in to hug the girl.

Jackson stood, probably to walk her to the door. She didn't need that. She didn't need any of this.

"I'll see myself out."

Jackson walked with her anyway. "You'll be back?"

"Yes, Jackson, I'll be back."

He must have read her mind.

"Thank you." He grinned as he opened the front door for her. "Sorry if I haven't been the best host. It isn't every day that I get a wake-up call like this one."

She didn't want to like Jackson Cooper. She didn't want to let her guard down. But he had a way of easing into a person's life, taking them by surprise.

"I think we've both been taken by surprise today."

Maybe she had been the most surprised. She had formed opinions about Jackson. Now she had to rethink those opinions.

Chapter Three

Jackson couldn't think of another reason to keep Madeline from leaving. He could think of several reasons why he wanted her to stay. She stood on his porch, brown hair, brown eyes, brown sweater and skirt. He couldn't quite figure her out, and he felt pretty sure that's what she planned when she camouflaged herself in brown. What she probably hadn't expected with her disguise was the fact that she intrigued him.

"I have to go." She stepped away from him, tripping over that crazy dog of his.

Jackson reached for her arm and steadied her. "Sorry about the dog. He can get in the way."

"Right, okay, I'll see you later."

"Madeline, thank you. I'm sure getting mixed up in this mess wasn't on your to-do list when you woke up this morning."

"No, it wasn't. And I'm still not sure how I feel about this. I think you should call family services."

"It's the right thing to do?" He smiled because he guessed she always went by the rules. "But then she's in the system and my hands are tied. I'd like to figure this out and then I'll make a phone call."

"She could be a runaway."

"I'm going to check into that. Don't worry, I'm not planning on harboring a juvenile."

Madeline's brows shot up. "I think you plan on letting me harbor said juvenile."

He grinned and shoved his hands into the front pockets of his jeans.

"If you go to jail, I'll bail you out."

"Thank you, that's very kind." She glanced at her watch. "I have to go. Please think about calling your parents."

The urge to lean down and kiss her cheek didn't come as a surprise. But today he had to think like Jackson the dad, not Jackson the guy who loved beautiful women. He smiled and promised her he'd think about calling his parents. But he'd already come to the conclusion that the last thing he needed was the entire Cooper clan descending on his house today.

Madeline hurried down the steps and across the lawn to her little sedan. He couldn't help but smile as she slammed the door, opened it and slammed it again before driving away. He remembered her doing that when he'd helped her pick up her groceries last week.

When he walked back inside he found Jade on the sofa, a throw blanket pulled over her body. She blinked, and offered a little smile.

"I guess you were up all night?" He eased down onto the desk chair he'd left in the middle of the room.

"Yeah, pretty much."

Jackson rolled the chair closer to her. "I'm going to get some work done. You take a nap and later we'll figure out what to do next."

"What's next? I'm your kid and my mom is dead.

What are you going to do, dump me on the side of the road somewhere?"

"No, I'm not going to dump you. I do want to check all of the facts before we make any big plans."

"Fine." She looked a little pale and her eyes were huge. "Do I have grandparents or something?"

"Yeah, you have grandparents."

She closed her eyes, a little-girl smile on her face. After a few minutes he scooted in the other direction, back to the desk and his laptop. He flipped the top up and hit the power button, all the while watching a kid who really thought he could be her dad.

He sighed and shook his head. First he checked his email because a certain bull he'd been after for a year had been put up for sale and he'd made an offer. Still nothing on that front.

So where did he begin searching for Jade Baker's story? And her mother's? Death records, obituaries and telephone directories. Every search came up empty. He had another connection, a friend who had gone into law enforcement. He typed a short email asking for information on runaways—one specific runaway, actually.

He sat back, trying to think of other avenues for finding Gloria Baker. But it wasn't her name he typed in the search engine of the internet. He found himself doing a search for Madeline Patton.

She'd been in the area for a year. She'd moved to a town where she didn't have family. She'd bought a house connected to his land. The house had once belonged to his great-grandparents. It had been their original homestead, before oil and ranching paid off for the Coopers.

His grandmother had taken a liking to Madeline and sold that little house and two acres to the schoolteacher for almost nothing. Maybe his grandmother knew more about her than the rest of them.

Or maybe he was the only Cooper left out of the loop when it came to Madeline. That kind of bugged him.

His search of Madeline Patton turned up article after article, all from Montana newspapers. He leaned back in his chair and his finger hovered above the mouse. Her story, if she had one, should be private. But the brief sentence under the heading wouldn't let him back away. He clicked the link and started reading.

For a long time he sat there. He read newspaper articles about a child named Madeline Patton. He searched for more articles. As he read he went from pain to rage. He had never wanted to hurt someone as badly as he did at that moment, thinking about that little girl.

Man, it made him want to drive to the school and hug her tight. It made him want to keep her safe. No one should ever be used the way Madeline had been used. Exploited. Hurt.

He closed down his computer because he knew these were her stories, her secrets. She had a right to her privacy. She didn't trust him. She definitely wouldn't trust him with these secrets.

He stood, easing through the motion and then holding on to the desk as he took a deep breath. Jade remained curled in a ball on his sofa, sound asleep. He leaned over her, shaking her shoulders lightly. Eyes opened with a flutter and she pulled back.

"I have to get some work done in the barn. Are you going to be okay here by yourself?" He figured being by herself might be something she was used to. Just guessing.

"Yeah, I'm still tired."

"Sleep on. If you get hungry there's lunch meat in

the fridge and a container of chili my mom brought over yesterday."

"Thanks." Her eyes closed.

Jackson slipped on his boots and pulled on a jacket. When he stepped outside he took a deep breath of cold, December air. It felt good to get out of the house. He never would have made it in the nine-to-five corporate world. Walls were not his cup of tea. He liked open spaces, horses in the field and bulls moving around their pens.

Blake, his older and less charming brother, could have the corporate gig. If someone had to count the money, it might as well be Blake.

Jackson whistled for the dog. He came running from the field, brown splotches on his back where he'd been rolling in the grass. When the dog got close enough, Jackson groaned.

"Bud, you stink. Get out of here."

Bud wagged his tail as if being stinky sounded like a compliment.

He shrugged down into his jacket and trudged down the driveway toward the barn. Horses whinnied and trotted along the fence line. Cattle started moving from across the field.

He flipped on lights in the barn and a few whinnies greeted him. He stopped in front of the stall of the little mare he'd bought last week. She stuck her velvety black nose over the door of the stall and he rubbed her face. She'd make some pretty foals. Her daddy had sired quite a few champion cutting horses. Her brother was a champion barrel horse. If people were concerned about pedigrees, hers topped the charts.

A minute later he walked on down the aisle to the feed room. As he unhooked the door he heard a truck easing down the driveway, the diesel engine humming, tires crunching on gravel. He stepped back to the center of the aisle and shook his head. Travis, late as usual.

As much as he loved his kid brother, Jackson missed Reese. They were closer in age and understood each other a little better. But Reese was deployed to Afghanistan and wouldn't be home for a year.

It was going to be a long year. He'd be doing a lot of praying during that time. He and God would be on pretty good terms by the time Reese came home.

Travis whistled a country song as he walked through the wide doors of the stable. He was tall and lanky, his light brown hair curled like it hadn't seen a brush in days. Nothing slowed Travis down. And nothing ever seemed to get him down.

"I didn't expect to see you up and around today." Travis pulled on leather work gloves.

"Is that why you waited until noon to feed?" Jackson blew out a breath, letting go of his irritation.

"Had a cow down and had to pull a calf. I knew everyone here had plenty of hay until I could get here. And I also know you well enough to know you can't stand staying down."

"Yeah, I feel better."

"Good, but let's not go crazy, right?" Crazy, as in give himself a chance to heal.

"Right." Jackson scooped grain into a bucket and headed for the first stall. They were only five horses in the stable; the rest were in the pasture. There were two stallions, a gelding he was training for a guy in Oklahoma City, a mare that had been brought over for an introduction to his stallion, Dandy, and the little black mare.

"You left your front door open." Travis stopped to

pet the black mare. "You really think this mare is going to throw some nice foals? She's small."

"She's fast."

He didn't remember leaving the door open and wondered if Jade had woken up. Fortunately Travis let it go. He grabbed a bale of hay and tossed it in a wheelbarrow without asking more questions. He pushed the wheelbarrow down the aisle, whistling again, and Jackson knew he wasn't getting off the hook that easily. Travis didn't let go of anything. But for now he seemed to be content with a nonanswer. He shoved two flakes of hay into the feeders on the stalls. When he got to the stallion, Dandy, he pulled off three flakes.

"Don't overfeed him." Jackson warned.

Travis grinned. "He's a big guy doing a lot of work. He requires extra fuel."

"Not every feeding."

"I'm not five." Travis pushed the wheelbarrow back to the hay stacked in the open area between stalls. He piled on two bales for the horses outside.

"I know you're not." But it was hard to turn off "big brother" mode. He'd been getting Travis out of scrapes for over twenty years.

"The charity bull ride for Samaritan House is next week. Do you think you'll be able to go?" Travis was a bull fighter, the guy responsible for distracting bulls as the bull rider made a clean getaway. Or distracting bulls when the getaway wasn't clean. Sometimes the bull fighter took a direct hit to keep the rider safe. That made him a hero. Travis had taken more than his share of hits.

Jackson slapped his little brother on the back. "I'm going to take a rain check."

Travis grinned. "Really? What's going on with you?"

as still noticeable, even after
and being raised as a Cooper.
e if I'll be able to make it. If

e."

he sun was bright and the sky
n sight. It hadn't warmed up
be heading in that direction.

of their best bulls. Jackson
pe enclosure and raised a foot
pe of the six-foot-tall pen. He
sionally for several years. He
s hauled them and then sold
eeding program was his baby.
en Reese and Travis, was the

had become a big business,
ought it would be.

gy, Holstein mix bull. "Bottle
the championship round in

m had guessed that little bull
would be a champion bucking
wing at the ground and look-
top athlete and not the sickly
s earlier.

drive. Jackson didn't turn as
a week ago. Travis beat him
meant a lot of explaining for

tton?" Travis crossed his arms
he fence but turned to watch
e car and then the front door

What in the world was she doing here so early?

"Yeah, I guess it is." Jackson turned his back to the woman and kid heading their way. He needed to think fast and distract Travis.

But of course this would be the day that Travis was focused and sharp. He pulled dark-framed glasses out of his pocket and shoved them onto his handsome face. Somehow Travis always looked studious in those glasses. And serious.

Jackson kept his own attention focused on Bottle Rocket.

"So, Madeline Patton and a kid that looks like you. Something you want to tell me?" Travis stared straight ahead, his voice low.

Jackson wanted to clobber his younger brother. Travis was like the farm dog that kept chewing up shoes, but you kept it anyway. He didn't mean to cause trouble, he just naturally found it.

"No, I don't really have much to tell you."

"Well, there are rumors spreading through town about a kid that looks like you showing up at the Mad Cow asking for directions to Jackson Cooper's house."

Travis let out a sigh and shook his head. He stepped back from the fence and turned to face the woman and teenager heading their way.

"People in this town gossip more than they pray." Jackson walked away from his younger brother.

"Shoot, Jackson, what do you think a prayer chain is?"

Jackson didn't wait for Travis, but Travis caught up with him anyway, "Travis, I'd hope that a prayer chain is for prayer."

"Is she yours?"

Jackson glanced at Travis. "What do you think?"

"What are you going to do about it?"

Jackson shrugged. At this point he didn't have a clue. But it would help if he could find her mother. Since he'd discovered there wasn't a death certificate for Gloria Baker, he assumed she was still alive.

Chapter Four

Madeline didn't quite know what to say, not with Travis staring from Jackson to Jade and then to her. She wanted to lift her hands and back away. She wanted to explain to them all that this family drama didn't belong to her. But the girl standing next to her, what happened to her if Madeline took the quickest exit from the situation?

Common sense told her that someone else would step in. If she left, Jackson would have to turn to his family for help. She looked up, caught him watching her, probably wondering the same thing she'd caught herself wondering. Why in the world was she here? He grinned and winked.

Someday she'd regret this moment, the moment she decided not to walk away. But the past had to be conquered. She couldn't spend her life running from the fear. Standing there looking at Jackson Cooper, all of that fear, rational and irrational, rushed in, pummeling her heart.

She took a deep breath and Jade reached for her hand, holding her in that spot.

"Travis, maybe it's time for you to go." Jackson

on the back. "And if you can,

'Will do, brother. If I can."

e walked away. Madeline
she couldn't ignore Jackson
front of her, an imposing six
nd charm.

reating back as she followed
adeline fought back the urge
, was easy. Something had
ces a few weeks ago, about
rength, not our own. If she
r own, she could be strong,
ith God.

isn't easy. I think the sooner
etter."

It isn't as if I'm a kid who's
l his dad he messed up. I've
fe, Madeline. I know exactly

she didn't know him or what
be charming and funny. He
her spilled canned goods. He
hen a neighbor needed help.
ad been an example of that.
n homes that were damaged.
er to people trying to rebuild

ut him. Admired him from a
nce kept a person safe.

, Jackson." The words slipped
mbarrassing once they were

said. She looked away, seeking Jade, making sure the girl hadn't decided to climb on a bull or a wild horse.

Jackson stared at her for a long minute and then he smiled.

"Madeline, I think that's about the nicest thing anyone has ever said to me."

"I doubt that. But honestly, about Jade…"

He glanced at his watch. "What are you doing here so early?"

"We got out at noon today. I forgot to tell you that earlier."

"Right, a holiday?"

"For the kids. A planning day for teachers." She started toward the barn, drawn by the whinny of a horse and laughter. Jackson walked next to her. She glanced up at him. "What are you going to do?"

"I'm not sure. I can't find any information on her mother's death. And I emailed a friend in law enforcement. She hasn't been reported missing."

Madeline stopped walking. "So where do you think her mother is?"

He didn't have a clue. "Maybe she's the one that's missing? I might have to drive to Enid. I'm going to keep searching because I'm starting to think she's not actually from Enid."

"You think?"

"What, you came to that conclusion first?"

She smiled because the look on his face said he clearly didn't think she could think of it first. "The thought had crossed my mind. I think there's far more to her story than she's telling."

"The guy is always the last to know." He motioned her inside the stable ahead of him.

Madeline loved barns of all kinds, but this one took

melling of hay and horses, it
a wide aisle that led into the
ayed softly and Jade stood in
retty black mare.

kson, hazel eyes glittery and
itiful horse."

n walked up next to the girl.
ll let you ride her."

orse." Jade's voice came out

ng we'll take care of." Jackson
ne and she felt a little wistful,
s. Patton?"

es with Andie Johnson."

n the horse who had her head
Vhy don't you have a Christ-

rapid change of topics. Mad-
use he clearly needed to adjust
ain worked. He didn't under-
could have a dozen or more
nd at once.

need one."

at that revelation. "You have
How can you have Christmas

Because I go to my parents'
e."

to jump in but Jade turned,
her in.

Jade asked, her attention now

itiful, really. She had a pink

tree with silver ornaments. It had seemed like a good idea at the time because it came pre-decorated.

Now a pink Christmas tree just seemed wrong.

"Christmas isn't about a tree." Jackson stepped in, almost defensive.

Jade blew out, obviously disgusted. "I think I know that. The tree isn't what Christmas is all about, but it kind of makes me think more about the holiday."

"We'll get a tree." Jackson herded them toward the door of the barn. "Tomorrow."

Madeline thought about tomorrow, the day she planned on baking bread, decorating her house and then working on finishing touches at the Dawson Community Center's living nativity. She also needed to run to town and buy ingredients for candy.

"We can drive my truck out to the back pasture and find a decent cedar. And if Madeline needs a tree, we can cut her one, too."

"I really don't." Madeline stiffened when his hand went to her back, lingered and then moved away. When she glanced at him his hands were in his pockets and his smile had disappeared.

"Of course you do." He looked down at her. "We'll cut down trees and then we'll come back here for hot chocolate and cookies."

Jade's face lit up. "Perfect."

Madeline wanted to disagree. Perfect would be how she'd describe her life before this morning, before being invaded by the two Coopers standing next to her. Perfect would be her little pink tree being left alone and her heart not hammering out the tune "Meet Me Under the Mistletoe."

She didn't want those thoughts, those dangerous-to-her-heart thoughts. She didn't want to be afraid. Of what, she asked herself. Afraid of rejection? Afraid he'd hurt her? Or worse.

Always worse.

God's strength. She reminded herself that she could do this, she could face her fears. She could be the strong person she sometimes knew existed inside her.

Tomorrow should be good enough to start on being strong. Today she had to deal with her emotions tumbling inside her, mocking her because she'd thought she had them locked up tight.

Jade and Jackson were still talking and laughing, discussing the plan for tomorrow. She wanted to explain that she already had plans. Instead she chose escape.

"I should go. I need to get some stuff done at my house before our big adventure tomorrow."

Jade walked away from the horse but her gaze lingered on the animal, and then turned to Jackson. Of course she wanted to stay with him. Madeline understood that. But Jade, like so many kids that Madeline knew who were used to disappointment, brushed it off. She raised her chin a notch, shrugged, and let it go.

Still, it had to hurt. Even if she knew how to pretend none of this bothered her, on the inside, where it counted, Madeline knew Jade had to be afraid.

Worse, she seemed to be counting on Madeline for strength and for guidance.

"What are you going to do for the rest of the day?" Jackson leaned against a stall door and she figured it had to be holding him up.

"Is there something you need?"

He grinned and winked. "A back rub would be good. Are you offering?"

"Do you ever stop?"

His smile faded. "Yeah, I do. I'm sorry for saying

that. You might have to give me a few days to get the old Jackson under control."

"Right, of course."

"Do you think you'll be going to town today?" Jackson reached into his back pocket and pulled out his wallet.

"I had planned on picking up Christmas decorations in Grove. Why?"

"Because I thought I'd give you money for groceries since you've got another mouth to feed. And she might need some clothes and a warmer coat."

"I'm fine. You don't have to worry about me." Jade moved to stand next to Madeline, her shoulders squared and stiff. "I'm good at taking care of myself."

"I'm sure you are, Jade, but that isn't necessary. You came looking for a family and this is what family does." Jackson handed Madeline several bills and she folded the money and put it in her pocket.

"I can take her." Madeline smiled at the girl standing next to her. "We can have fun shopping."

Jade shrugged slim shoulders. "Okay, sure. So I'm leaving and I won't see you until tomorrow?"

After a long pause, Jackson eased closer, taking stiff steps that Madeline hadn't noticed earlier. She wondered if he was even supposed to be up, let alone doing chores.

"Jade, I want to spend time with you. We're going to figure this whole mess out and I'm going to do my best to help you…"

"I don't need help. I need a dad."

His features softened. "I know, and I'm going to do my best to help you with that. But honestly, kid, I need to crash. I think my ribs are about to snap in two and my back kind of feels like a truck is sitting on it.

Now that isn't the toughest 'dad' kind of thing to admit. Especially in front of two women." He smiled a tight smile. "But that's the way it is."

"Fine." Jade stood on tiptoe and kissed his cheek.

And something about him changed. Madeline watched his eyes and face shift and suddenly, Jackson Cooper became a dad. Or at least what she always imagined a dad would be if she'd had a real one.

"We should go." Madeline reached for Jade. "What time tomorrow? And are you sure you don't want me to bring something over for dinner tonight?"

"I think by nine in the morning." Jackson winked at Jade before turning to smile at Madeline. "And don't worry about me. I'm going to crash, and food is the last thing I want."

They walked back to the house together, slowly. Jackson watched them get in the car and then he eased his way up the steps of the front porch and into the house. Madeline waited until he stepped through the door before she shifted into Reverse.

"You think he's cute, don't you?"

Madeline blinked a few times at the crazy question the teenager sitting next to her had asked. Jade smiled at what Madeline had hoped would be a warning look. Maybe she needed to work on that.

"Jackson doesn't need for anyone to think he's cute. He thinks it enough about himself."

"Mmm-hmm."

Let it go, her wise inner voice said. *Let it go.* She drove on down the road, back to her house. When they reached her place she pulled up to the mailbox.

"Could you reach in and get my mail?" She pulled close and rolled the window down for Jade.

"Sure." Jade reached into the box and pulled out

a few pieces of mail. Rather than handing it over she sifted through it. "Hey, a Christmas card from Marjorie Patton. Is that your sister or your mom?"

Madeline grabbed the mail and shoved it in her purse. "It's no one."

Jackson woke up in a dark living room, the dog at his feet growling. He groaned and tossed the pillow across the room. Twice in one day. In one long, long day. The doorbell chimed again and he pushed himself off the couch, groaning as he straightened, stretching the muscles in his back.

Things to do tonight: sleep in own bed.

"I'm coming, already."

He threw the door open and immediately backed down. "Sir."

His dad stood in the doorway, the look on his face a familiar one. At almost thirty-four, Jackson should be long past that look from anyone. But there it was, the "buddy, you're in big trouble" look.

"Come in, I'll put on a pot of coffee."

Tim Cooper stomped the mud off his boots and stepped inside the house. "Smells like dog in here."

"Yeah, the stupid dog refuses to sleep outside. Either he's worried about me, or he just doesn't like the cold. I'm going with the cold."

"Probably. You're walking like you're eighty years old."

"Yeah, well, I feel older than that."

"What spooked that horse? Did you ever figure it out?"

They reached the kitchen and Jackson motioned for his dad to sit down while he filled the water reservoir on the coffeemaker and pushed the power button.

"I think it was a loose door banging in the wind. We both know that isn't why you're here."

"I can be here for more than one reason. Your mom is worried because she tried to call and you didn't answer."

"I was dog-tired."

"I told her you were probably asleep."

Jackson reached for the bottle of painkillers on the counter and then he put them back. It wasn't so bad he couldn't walk it off. "And the other reason you're here?"

"Travis has a big mouth."

"Right, I figured as much. Something about the words 'Travis, keep your mouth shut' tends to loosen his mouth like an oiled hinge."

His dad kind of laughed. He took his hat off and sat it on the table. "She isn't yours?"

"Probably not." Jackson sat down next to his dad. He fiddled with the stack of mail he'd left on the table earlier that day. "But my name is on her birth certificate."

"Where's her mom?"

"Your guess is as good as mine." Jackson got up to make the coffee. He put a cup under the nozzle. "Black?"

"Yeah. Oh, your mom sent dinner. It's in the truck and I'll bring it in before I leave."

"Thanks. You know, I'll never learn to cook if she keeps feeding me."

"She isn't going to stop. I've tried. And she's itching to fix this situation for you, too."

Jackson set the two cups of coffee on the table. "I'll fix this myself. The fewer people involved the better."

"I don't think your mom thinks that she's one of the

people who shouldn't be involved. She said to tell you she'll expect to see you tomorrow."

"Give me a few days. I'm trying to figure this out without hurting Jade."

"Is that her name?"

He nodded and took a sip of coffee. "Yeah, Jade Baker. I knew her mom. But you know…"

"Yeah. Might need to head to the doctor just to make sure."

"I will. I'm not turning her out in the cold. I'm not going to call the state yet. I'm not going to have her in the system at Christmas."

"Where is she?"

This is where it got tricky. He sipped his coffee and gave himself a minute. His dad answered his own question.

"Travis said Madeline Patton was up here today."

"She was."

"Madeline, huh?" Tim grinned kind of big, the way a man did when he'd raised a bunch of sons. "Not your normal cup of tea."

"I've never been a tea person."

"No, you haven't." Tim lifted his cup and finished off his coffee. "Don't hurt her. If you don't want big trouble with your mother, remember that people think of lot of Madeline."

"I'm not chasing the schoolteacher, if that's what you think." He shook his head. "And I'm not eighteen years old. So thanks for the advice."

Tim stood. He put a hand on Jackson's shoulder. "She's the kind of woman a guy marries."

Yeah, that said it all. Put him in his place. Jackson, who had done his running around and then settled down on this farm with a dog and some livestock, had

n. It sure felt like he couldn't
undo what the people around

lad out of the kitchen, and he
mpt at denial. "I'm not plan-
atton."

en do things ever go the way

s helping with Jade."
slapped Jackson on the back.
ver usually leads right where
;o."

front porch, thinking of all
It wasn't until his dad's tail-
e remembered his dinner in

is appetite.

Chapter Five

A light snow had fallen overnight, just enough to dust the grass and the trees. Madeline drove her car up the long driveway to Jackson Cooper's ranch. The old farmhouse with the wraparound porch looked pretty with the powdery white snow sprinkling down. In the field the cows stood tail to the wind, snow sticking to their thick winter coats.

"This sure ain't Oklahoma City," Jade whispered.

"What? And don't say 'ain't.'" Madeline pulled her car in at the side of the house.

"Nothing. And I'm sorry." Jade already had her door open. "I bet he's still sleeping."

"No, he isn't. I saw him walk out of the barn."

"Oh, okay." Jade slammed the door of the Buick and ran toward the big barn.

Madeline waited. And she worried. What happened to a girl when she thought she'd found a fairytale parent who would make everything right, and then found herself let down? Heartache? Madeline remembered a father, but he hadn't been her real father. She blocked the memory because too many other memories chased after it. Yesterday she'd gotten a card from her

ged to find her. Mad-
fast enough to outrun
e the past.

or letters. Usually she
e last time. No matter
or said she wouldn't
nce to talk, Madeline

see had disappeared
earched for her sister
Jackson. She hadn't
ried. Or changed her
that option years ago,

She didn't know how
felt as if she had to
ne and become some-
ed to her. Not that she
ould be a great way to

ahead but she turned
erself.

d. She followed at a
d about spending the
him. It exhausted her
oo much energy and

her way. The dog ran
ith her, nipping at her

We're going to get a
r her hand.
es out here."

"Right, that makes it more like Christmas."

Jackson walked out of the barn, smiling and waving when he saw them. "I have everything we need in the truck. I'll get it."

"Coffee?" Madeline shivered inside her coat. When she looked up, met his gaze, he smiled. And then he let his gaze drop.

"Where's the schoolteacher?" He winked at Jade.

"What does that mean?" Madeline looked down at herself and then up at him.

He moved his hands in circles. "You're in jeans. And you're not wearing your glasses."

Jade laughed, loud and silly. "I did it. I talked her into wearing jeans and putting in the contacts she never wears. You can't chop down a Christmas tree in a skirt."

"I see." Jackson took a step closer. "Not a bad change, Maddie. Not bad at all."

"It's jeans and contact lenses." She shot him a look and he raised both hands in surrender, his smile fading. She pulled her heavy coat a little closer. "And my name's Madeline."

"You're right, it's just jeans and a new coat. People change clothes every day."

Jade raced into the barn. A second later she ran back out, her face beaming. "It's a wagon, Madeline, a real wagon."

The pumpkin will be your coach, Cinderella. Make sure you're home by midnight.

She grimaced and pushed fairy tales from her mind as she walked into the barn to see what had Jade jumping up and down this time. The girl went from defiant and strong-willed to giddy in the blink of an eye.

Maybe changing with the ease of a chameleon was

a Cooper trait and the girl had gotten it from Jackson. Hazel eyes, blond hair and the ability to shake off pain and become someone else.

As they walked through the open double doors of the barn, Jackson touched her arm, his hand cupping her elbow. "It's a Cooper tradition. I know we aren't going with the family, but I thought we should do this the right way."

A buckboard wagon pulled by two honey-colored horses stood in the wide center aisle of the barn. The harness jangled as the two large animals nodded their heads up and down, chewing on the metal bits in their mouths.

"I told you." Jade ran to the back and started to climb in. The dog jumped around her feet, happy, it seemed, to have someone in his life who could be easily excited.

"Climb in." Jackson led her to the front of the wagon, indicating with a nod the little step and a handle on the side of the wagon.

"We're really going off into the field in a wagon."

"We really are." He put a hand on her waist.

Her hand froze in midair, inches short of the handle as his touch lingered. She closed her eyes and exhaled. Pleasure and fear mixed like some crazy concoction that made her brain fuzzy and her heart ache.

The woman in her wanted to know that someone could find her attractive, someone could see how special she was. Someone could want to love her. She wanted to believe someone could melt her heart and make her feel whole.

She wasn't sweet sixteen and never been kissed. She was twenty-eight, and in the arms of a man she'd never felt more than distance and the wild urge to escape.

The child in her, that little girl that had hidden in

closets and tried to run, wanted to escape because this man shook her heart, and because another man had made her feel dirty to the depth of her soul.

And it had taken years of counseling to get past that pain.

It had taken a faith that renewed and taught forgiveness to get her past the hatred. She still needed to work on the part of the plan that said she could love herself.

She had never let a man inside her heart because she'd never wanted to feel that pain again. She never wanted to be betrayed again.

Jackson stood behind her, his hand still light on her waist. Jade laughed and played with the dog, unaware. Jackson stepped closer.

"I'm just helping you in the wagon, Maddie."

She nodded and his hand moved to her back as she stepped up and into the wagon. As she settled into the seat he led the horses from the barn. She ducked as they went through the door, but there wasn't really a need. In the back, Jade had settled under a blanket with Bud the dog.

Jackson, stern in a way she'd never seen him, tipped his hat to her and then walked around and climbed up next to her. They didn't speak as the wagon started on a worn trail toward an already open gate.

He had nothing to say and her heart seemed to be tripping all over itself, trying to catch up with twenty-eight years of emotions and new revelations about herself.

She folded her hands in her lap as the wagon bumped and jostled along the trail. No cattle or horses grazed in the field they were traveling through. The winter morning was cold and quiet. Even Jade seemed to be too excited to talk. For once.

Madeline found herself wanting to talk nonstop. For once. Talking would be easier than the silence, easier than delving into that moment back in the barn. A moment when she'd wondered what it would be like to turn into his arms, to be held by him.

She nearly laughed at that thought. What would Jackson Cooper do if a church mouse like her threw herself at him? A smile crept across her face. He'd die of shock. He'd run for his life.

He surely wouldn't know what to do.

Not that women didn't pursue him. But Madeline Patton in pursuit would probably scare ten years off his life. It scared ten years off hers just thinking about it.

"Here we go." Jackson pulled the team up and set the handbrake on the wagon. Jade hurried to stand, wobbling and grabbing the back of the bench seat he and Madeline were sitting on.

"What are you two waiting for?" She hopped over the side, the dog, Bud, jumping after her.

"We're coming." Jackson glanced at the woman next to him. She'd been quiet the whole trip out. Not that fifteen minutes of silence was impossible for a woman, but he thought her silence said everything she wasn't willing to say.

He wasn't about to push his way into her life, to tell her she didn't have to be afraid, that he wouldn't hurt her.

He had hurt women, not intentionally, but because he hadn't ever been the guy that wanted to take a few dates and turn them into something more. Yeah, she was smart to keep her distance from someone like him.

But if he was going to have a cup of tea…

Crazy thought. He wasn't a tea-drinking man.

"We should get down." He said it smooth and easy, as if he hadn't just been having thoughts that shook him from his comfort zone.

Last summer he'd teased Wyatt Johnson about Rachel Waters, telling Wyatt that the woman would get under his skin. And he'd been right. They were married now and as happy as any two people could be.

He knew better than to let a woman get under his skin. Even one as sweet as Madeline Patton, with her quiet ways and soft smiles.

She looked up at him; her mouth opened as if she meant to say something. Probably something he didn't want to hear. He didn't think she would be the type to call a man names, but he'd been called a few in his life.

"Thank you."

That was it. And he didn't even know why she was thanking him. Before he could question her she hopped down out of the wagon and walked away. Her new coat was brick red. It was a crazy combination with her brown hair hanging loose and the wind blowing it around her face. Her boots left tiny prints in the light dusting of snow. She turned to look back at him, catching her hair back from her face with her hand.

"You going to join us?"

Yeah, he was joining them. He stepped down out of the wagon, landing with a jolt that shot through his pancreas or something. He took a deep breath and whistled as he exhaled.

"You okay?" Madeline called back.

"Yeah, I'm good." Great. Wonderful. Happy.

He grabbed the chain saw out of the back of the wagon and followed the two ladies on a merry chase for the "perfect" tree.

"You know there isn't a perfect tree, right?" He trudged along behind them, smiling a little as they circled a tree close to twelve feet high.

"What do you call this?" Jade turned and then she started singing, "Oh Christmas tree, oh Christmas tree."

"I call this too big for my house." He walked on and they followed after him.

"Scrooge," Madeline whispered as she moved past him.

"You'd better believe it." He snorted and she laughed. And he wondered if she realized how much fun she was having. "So how'd it go last night?"

She stopped and her gaze remained on Jade who had skipped away with the dog to survey a tree she'd seen and it had to be the one.

"She's a mess." Madeline smiled and started walking again. "And now my house is a mess. I think you need a turn at the trail of clothes, water on the bathroom floor and dishes on the counter."

"And deny you the pleasure?"

She sighed and didn't laugh. "Seriously, Jackson, her mom has to be out there somewhere. We can't keep her here forever."

"I know that. I've got someone working on it. I'll find her."

"And then what?" Madeline looked up at him, her brown eyes locking with his. "Send her back? What if it isn't a safe situation? What if…"

Jackson got it. "What if you get attached and can't stand to let her go?"

Madeline shrugged. "She's heading back."

"Right, of course. And you're very good at skipping out on answering questions."

"What, are you going to tell me you won't get attached? Or that you won't worry? I know relationships are easy for you. Are they that easy to walk away from?"

Jackson stopped, stunned, and more than a little mad. "That's a great assessment from someone who doesn't really know me."

"I'm sorry." She reached for his arm. "That was unfair."

"A little." Not too much. The old saying that the truth hurt might have worked for this situation. Not that he planned on telling her that bit of information.

"This is it!" Jade pointed to the biggest cedar on the place. It had to be twenty feet. "It's perfect."

"Really? Perfect for what, the White House? Let's see if we can't find something a little smaller."

She did the teenage eye roll and walked on. He didn't have a single parenting bone in his body. He was a fraud. The only thing he knew to do was mimic things he'd heard his dad say over the years.

"What about this one?" Madeline pointed to a medium-size tree.

"Hmm, yes, it's good. It isn't very full. It doesn't have huge open gaps." Jade walked around the tree. "Yes, this is good. And we need one for Madeline's."

"No, we don't have to do that." Madeline shot him a look.

He remembered his sister Mia, when someone would offer her something that she thought was too much and she didn't want to be a bother. He smiled at the memory.

"Of course you need a tree." A kid in his life for twenty-four hours and he'd suddenly turned into his dad.

Maybe he'd wake up and this would be a dream. Or a strange version of *It's a Wonderful Life*. This was his world invaded by domesticity. He could almost hear the angel, Clarence, telling him that his life would be better with a family. Without them his home was empty, quiet.

Now how was peace and quiet such a bad thing?

"I really don't need one." Madeline had already spotted one. He knew it the minute she smiled.

"That one, right there. The small one?"

She nodded and smiled at him. "Please."

"You got it, Maddie."

She didn't correct him this time.

He left the chain saw on the ground and picked up the handsaw he'd brought. It would take about five minutes to cut through the trunk of a little bitty cedar. The part he'd forgotten about was the kneeling down part. That meant him on the ground, cracked ribs and all, pushing a saw back and forth. Through one of the toughest little cedars he'd ever seen.

By the time he finished the second tree, standing up just about wasn't an option.

He backed up, on his hands and knees, inhaling through the sharp pain. Jade had hold of her tree and started dragging it toward the wagon. Madeline stood in front of him.

"Need help?" She didn't smile.

"I'm afraid to admit that I do." He sat back up, moving into a squatting position that proved to be pretty overrated.

She stood there a long moment and then she reached for his hands. He made it to his feet, holding on to her as he stretched and the muscles in his back relaxed. Briefly.

"Phew, that was fun."

She was still holding his hands. She looked up, her eyes wide and deep-down hurt, the kind that took years to heal. Inside those dark eyes of hers he saw the little girl she'd been. He wanted to wrap her in his arms and protect her. He wanted to promise no one would ever hurt her again.

He let go of her hands because he wouldn't be the guy that broke her heart. She needed someone safe and dependable. How was that for being the grown-up, responsible guy? He'd have to share this moment with his dad.

The day Jackson Cooper used self-control.

What in the world had happened to him? Had he grown a conscience? Changed? Maybe all of those prayers uttered at Dawson Community Church on his behalf were suddenly being answered.

He chuckled.

"What?" Madeline had backed away, as if she'd suddenly come to her senses.

"Nothing, just thinking about prayers said on my behalf."

"What does that mean?"

"Are you going to say you haven't heard my mother or grandmother stand up in church and spill their guts about my life and how I need to come back to God?"

"That isn't really something to joke about." Madeline's eyes narrowed and he felt very chastised, for a second.

"I'm not joking. I know what they say. I grew up in church."

"They don't gossip about you, if that's what you think. They love you and worry about you."

He smiled at her ruffled feathers. "I know. But I'm not so far from God as they all think. I pray. I read my Bible. I'm not dating a different woman every night of the week. I've hardly dated at all in the last six months." As if she really needed all this information.

They walked side by side back to the wagon. Jackson had pulled on his gloves and he dragged the bigger tree behind him. Madeline stopped him a short distance from the wagon. She put a hand on his arm.

"Why don't you go to church?"

He shrugged. "Got out of the habit, I guess. Years of running around, rodeoing, sowing those wild oats. God and I are working it out."

"I see. So when they ask for prayers for you on Sunday, should I tell them you're good?"

He grinned. "One of these days I'll show up and prove it myself."

"That would be nice. You know it breaks your mother's heart that you're not in church."

"I'm not the only one."

"I know. She wants all of her children in church with her."

"Have you always gone to church?" He lifted the cedar tree and tossed it into the back of the wagon. Jade had a stick and she tossed it for Bud to fetch. He watched her for a minute, wondering how much of her story was true. She didn't seem to be a heartbroken kid. Instead she acted as if she might be on the adventure of a lifetime.

"She's a cute kid."

"Yeah, she is." What in the world should he do with her? He couldn't just move a kid into his house and be her dad. He hadn't been sitting around his house thinking he wanted a kid cluttering up his bathroom, leaving dirty clothes on the floor and asking for money to go to the movies.

He watched her hug his dog when the heeler jumped up, front paws on her stomach. Truth time. He'd been thinking a lot lately about how empty his life had become.

"She's just looking for a family." Madeline's voice sounded wistful to him.

"I know."

"She admitted she researched your family when she found the birth certificate. A real family, that's what she wanted."

"So where is her mom?"

Madeline looked from the girl to him. "Try Oklahoma City."

"Gotcha." He whistled, and Bud came running back. Jade loped after him, her cheeks red from running and playing in the cold.

"Time to go?" She looked in the back of the wagon. "Where do I ride?"

"Up here with us."

She grinned big and climbed into the seat. He stood behind Madeline and waited for her to get situated and then he climbed up, sitting next to her. They were pushed together by Jade on the end of the bench seat.

Madeline swallowed, he saw her throat bob, saw a flicker of a pulse in her neck. If ever a woman needed a man who would make her feel safe, it was this one.

She needed a Prince Charming, someone like his brother Blake. Yeah, Blake wouldn't hurt a woman. He'd set her up in a nice house at the edge of Dawson. He'd buy her a pretty diamond ring and bring her flowers. Blake was a cold fish, though. For good reasons, Jackson figured, but still, his big brother needed to learn how to let go.

He'd have to do one better than that for Madeline. She needed someone. He smiled down at her. But not him.

Chapter Six

The horses picked up the pace on the way back to the barn. Their easy trot jangled the harness. Madeline sat sandwiched between Jade and Jackson. She shivered, not because of the cold, but because of him. She closed her eyes and breathed in the cold air.

Jackson drove the team past the barn and to the front door of the house. "I'll unload the tree and take the horses back to the barn."

"Where are your decorations?" Jade nearly bounced from the seat as they pulled up to the house and the team came to a jarring halt.

Madeline grabbed the girl and held her in the seat.

Next to her, Jackson pushed his hat back a notch. "Well now, that's a good question. I guess I hadn't thought about decorations."

"You have to **have** decorations," Jade insisted, hopping down from the wagon and joining the dog who had already done the same.

"No, not really. I haven't put a tree up in years. Let's take it inside and when I go to the barn I'll look in the storage shed."

Jackson eased himself down from the wagon, not as

quickly as before. Madeline filed away that information about him, because it changed who he was in her mind. Jackson Cooper, selfless? Willing to put himself through all kinds of agony in order to ensure a child had a Christmas tree?

He was the man holding his hand out, offering help getting down from the wagon. She could refuse and do it herself, looking stubborn and a little silly. Or rude. She could take his hand and risk everything.

Risk what? She bit down on her bottom lip and his hand still reached for hers. She nodded and stepped over the side of the wagon. His hand touched her waist, her arm. She landed gently on the ground. When she looked up it was into hazel eyes that danced with laughter.

Smile, she told herself, make it easy. Jackson Cooper dated tall, leggy blondes and polished brunettes. He didn't date mousy schoolteachers. She knew the drill. She would always fit the role of person most likely to help. She had always been the one a guy called if he thought she could help him hook up with someone else. And she had always liked filling that spot, because it didn't hurt so much if expectations were low. It didn't hurt if you didn't get too close.

As she stood there gathering herself, he opened his mouth as if he meant to say something. But he didn't.

"We'll make hot chocolate." She stepped away, turning to go inside.

"I'll be right back." He walked to the front of the wagon and took hold of the first horse in the team. "If you want hot chocolate there's a mix in the cabinet. Mom makes it every winter."

"Thank you." *Say something smart and witty*, she pushed herself. But she'd never been the smart, witty type. She'd never been the flirty one, batting her eyelids or saying cute things. She'd been the bookworm, hiding behind glasses and her studies.

She'd been the one hiding from life, protecting herself.

How in the world had this become her life? Laughter and a barking dog reminded her. A mix-up had dropped a child in her life and somehow tied her to Jackson Cooper. She could have dropped Jade off yesterday and driven away, not looking back, not thinking she had an obligation of any kind. Somewhere out there Jade, more than likely, had a mother who wanted her back.

"Let's go inside." She motioned for Jade as she walked up the steps.

As she walked through the front door of the house she did what she knew to do. She put all of her crazy emotions in a box and shoved them to the back of her mind.

"Do you think he has any cookies?" Jade followed behind her with the dog, who left muddy paw prints on the wood floor.

"I think the dog should stay outside." Madeline pointed to the paw prints.

Jade had already moved on. "Where should we put the tree?"

"It isn't my tree or my house so I'm not going to make that decision."

Jade glanced at her but didn't seem to be too bothered. "He wouldn't have a tree if it wasn't for us."

"I'm not even sure why I'm here," Madeline said out loud.

That got Jade's attention. The girl turned quickly, her eyes widening and her smile dissolving. "I'm sorry. I mean, I guess you probably have other things to do?"

"No, not really." She would have been at home knitting another scarf. She might have been cleaning her kitchen or reorganizing her cabinets. "Jade, where's your mom?"

Deflecting. Always safe. Not always fair.

Jade's eyes got huge and the color drained from her face. She walked away, the dog right on her heels.

"Jade?"

"It's none of your business. Remember, you're the person who got stuck with me. I came here looking for my dad and instead I'm staying with a lady who sleeps with every light in the house on."

The front door closed. "Problem here?"

Jackson walked into the living room, carrying a rubber tub with a lid. He'd shed his jacket and was dressed in jeans and a button-up shirt. If he felt the tension, he didn't show it. He took off his hat and hung it on a hook.

"No, there's no problem." She offered Jade an apologetic smile but the girl walked away.

"Let her go." Jackson said it in an easy, relaxed voice. "She'll get over it. She's too excited about the tree to stay mad for long."

"I asked where her mother is," Madeline admitted. "I thought she might talk to me."

"Talking isn't always easy."

"No, it isn't."

He pulled the lid off the box. "We could get you a dog."

"Excuse me?"

"It can't be cheap to have all of your lights on all the time."

She pulled out a string of lights that looked as if they

were from the last century. "What do you know about my lights?"

"I've driven by a few times and wondered."

"I'm fine."

He looked up, his hazel eyes asking questions she didn't want to answer.

"Are you really?"

The question made her wonder. Then she answered, and it didn't hurt, it wasn't a lie. "I really am."

Of course she had doubts. She did sleep with the lights on. But she'd come so far and she'd grown so much. But why did he ask? What did he know about her fear?

She didn't want his sympathy.

"We should go check on Jade." She backed away from him, but not fast enough. His hand shot out, stopping her escape.

"Jade's fine. She's rummaging through my cabinets and snooping through the kitchen. I'm getting you a dog."

She shook her head. "I don't need a dog."

"I'm either going to teach you to shoot a gun, or I'm getting you a dog."

"I don't really want either."

His hand still held her arm but he hadn't moved closer. "I know, but trust me on this. There's something kind of nice about coming home to a dog. It makes a house less lonely."

"I can get my own dog." It was her last attempt to hold on to independence and to take a stand against a man who had stormed her life as easily as Jade stormed his.

"I owe you for helping me out with Jade."

"I didn't have to help."

"No, you didn't." His hand slid down her arm to her hand. "But I'm glad you did."

"Jade," she whispered and glanced back over her shoulder.

"Right, Jade."

Jackson watched Madeline's retreat. He walked a little slower, giving her space, giving himself time to get his head together. What in the world was he thinking?

So she slept with the lights on. When had that become his problem? She'd been his neighbor for over a year. He said hello to her when they passed on the street or bumped into one another walking into the Mad Cow. He'd seen her lights on late at night, and he'd wondered about it. So now he knew and he thought he needed to buy her a dog to make her feel safe?

He needed his head examined.

Bachelor pad. That's what his house had been designed as. He walked into the kitchen and nearly groaned. The two females who had invaded his life were standing shoulder to shoulder mixing milk with his mother's cocoa mix. A plate of cookies had been set out on the counter. It smelled and looked like Sally Homemaker had moved in.

It smelled kind of nice, the combination of hot chocolate, cookies, popcorn and...Madeline's perfume. He leaned against the counter and watched the two of them have what looked like a mother-daughter moment.

"Did you find decorations?" Jade turned, a spoon in her hand. Her eyes sparkled and she smiled. Happy. And she wore it like new clothes, something she'd wanted and never had.

"Not much. I did find a couple of old tree stands.

One for mine, one for the tree you're taking to Madeline's."

Madeline looked at her watch. "I have to go soon."

"We have to decorate his tree." Jade stirred the cocoa and then lifted the spoon to take a sip. Madeline took the spoon from her hand and tossed it in the sink. Jade's mouth opened. "Why'd you do that?"

"I don't want to share germs."

"Fine." Jade grabbed another spoon and turned to Jackson again. "We can string the popcorn if you have a sewing kit around here. And maybe make some snowflakes."

"Sure, why not," he grumbled as he pulled cups from the cabinet. "Would you like to crochet doilies for my tables?"

Jade laughed and pointed to Madeline. "She can do that."

Madeline looked away, her cheeks turning crimson. The hot chocolate steamed and she ladled the liquid into the cups he'd set next to the stove.

"I bet she can." He grinned at Madeline's back because she had turned away from him and was pretending to be busy with the cocoa.

"We need to hurry," she finally said. "I have practice tonight."

"Cool. Can I go?" Jade leaned close to Madeline.

"I tell you what, we'll go do something this evening. Madeline has to practice for her part in the nativity. We'll let her do that and you and I will go somewhere."

"Together?" Jade's eyes lit up and her smile radiated.

"Yeah, together."

Madeline turned with a cup in her hand. She held it out to him and said nothing. She didn't need to. She needed a break from Jade. She needed a break from him. He got that. Sometimes he needed a break from himself.

They migrated to the living room with a tray of hot chocolate and cookies. Jade carried the popcorn and the miniature sewing kit he'd found in the cabinet. As they settled down to the task of making decorations, Jackson pushed the tree into the stand and picked up the string of lights.

He unfolded the ladder and headed to the top with lights and a pulled muscle in his back. Madeline looked up from cutting into folded paper to make a snowflake for his tree.

"You okay?" she asked, her eyes narrowing as she watched him.

He looked at the scene below him. A woman and a child making Christmas decorations. His floor strewn with craft paper and ornaments. It looked like a picture from a Christmas card, not a picture from his life. Maybe the life he could have had?

"Yeah, I'm good."

Thirty minutes later, with the creative talents of Jade and Madeline, the tree changed from the sad Charlie Brown tree they'd dragged in from the field into a real Christmas tree. Jade had even found a prize: a tiny bird's nest leftover from last year. She'd moved it from the inner branches and placed it front and center, filling it with tiny eggs made of colored paper.

"It looks good." He hadn't contributed much, just a star for the top and the string of lights. But it was a decent-looking tree, even with the big empty space on the side they'd pushed close to the wall.

"Now we have to decorate Madeline's tree," Jade proclaimed as she hung the last foil star. "She has real decorations."

"Hey, don't diss my tree." Jackson plugged in the lights. The strand of multicolored lights flickered and came on.

"I'm just saying." Jade smiled a cute kid smile. "Anyway, this is a good tree."

A knock on the door and they all froze. Madeline looked at him, then at Jade. Jackson shrugged and pointed at the dog who had decided to bark his fool head off. Bud sat down, tail wagging, but a menacing snarl still curled his lips.

"I'll be right back." Jackson touched Jade's head on the way to the door. "Stay in here."

When he opened the door a police officer stood on his front porch. Jackson stepped out the door and closed it behind him.

"Jackson, Douglas Clark called about the kid you have staying with you."

"She's not staying here. She's staying with Madeline Patton."

"I see. Can you tell me who she is and how she came to be here?"

"Well—" he paused because the only thing he had was Jade's birth certificate and her side of the story "—she's my daughter."

"Jackson, we need to clear this up. You have a minor who could be a runaway. That's not something we can turn our back on."

"I get that, Lance, but if she's my kid…"

"If she's not?"

"My name is on her birth certificate."

The officer started to get a grim look on his face. "Jackson, we need to try to contact her mother."

"Gotcha. What if I promise I'm trying to do that?

Look, I don't want the kid in state custody. Not this close to the holidays."

"Find her mom."

"I will." Jackson stood his ground in the door but Lance didn't turn to leave.

"Jackson, I have to talk to her."

"We're decorating the Christmas tree."

Lance laughed at that. Why did everyone find it so amusing when he did anything slightly different? "That's pretty domestic."

Jackson motioned Lance inside. They'd met on occasion, usually at a fire or an accident that volunteer first responders were called to. That was the thing about a small town, a rural county; people knew each other. They knew stories. They knew where to find someone without getting a map or directions.

Sometimes that could be a good thing. Sometimes it got under a guy's skin.

They walked into the now-empty living room. Empty except the twinkling, pitiful tree and leftover decorations scattered across the floor.

"She must be in the kitchen."

Lance nodded and walked next to him through the living room and dining room. When they entered the kitchen Jade turned, her eyes going all glittery with tears. Madeline moved closer and shot Jackson an accusing look.

"You called the police?" Jade trembled, her face draining of color.

"No," Jackson said. "Not this one."

"Young lady, I need your full name and address." Lance stood in a relaxed pose but his eyes shifted, taking in the room, the setting. Cop training. Jackson could have told him to relax, no one would jump out from behind a door. But that training kept a guy safe on the job.

Jade hiccupped a little.

"Jade, honey, tell him." Madeline, soft-voiced and sweet but still shooting daggers at Jackson.

Jackson should do something. He should step forward, put an arm around her. He'd been raised in a close family with parents that were always there for them, holding it together during the worst times.

Jackson tried to grab hold of those experiences. He might not be Jade's dad, but he could step up and be who she needed him to be. Tim Cooper had been the best dad in the world. He still was a man whose example could be followed.

"Give her a minute, Lance. She's a kid." Jackson stepped closer to Jade. "Go ahead. Tell him what he needs to know."

She nodded and wiped at her eyes. He put an arm around her shoulder and pulled her close for just a second and then released her. She smiled up at him and sniffled.

"I'm Jade Baker. My mom is Gloria Baker. We live in Oklahoma City."

"Your mom is alive?" Jackson had known, but he'd been willing to believe her until he found out the whole story.

Jade didn't answer. She cried. Tears slid down her cheeks and she shrugged.

"We need to contact your mother." Lance pulled a pen from his pocket. "Do you have her number?"

"Yeah, but good luck finding her."

"What does that mean?" Jackson leaned back against the counter, watching Jade shift from foot to foot. She looked up at him, tears pooling in her hazel eyes.

Man, he hated tears. He glanced at Madeline and her eyes were overflowing. Though he'd grown up with emotional females, he'd never gotten good at handling tears.

"Jade?" Madeline had the soft touch, the gentle voice that the kid needed. He shot her a grateful smile.

"She's never at home. She leaves for days at a time. The reason I came here is because I found my birth certificate and decided I'd find you and see if you were any better than her."

"Did you leave her a note?" Lance wrote on the pad and barely glanced up.

"Yeah, I left her a note. But she doesn't care where I go as long as I'm out of her hair. She's high most of the time and that's what she cares about, her next score and how to pay for it."

"Let's try to call her." Lance waited and Jade recited a number. He pulled out his cell phone and held it to his ear. After a few tries he gave up. "No answer."

"I told you." Jade looked down at the floor, at the dog sleeping at her feet. "I wanted a real Christmas with a real family."

"You're truant from school. You're a runaway." Lance ticked the crimes off on his fingers.

"I'm with my dad," Jade insisted and Jackson couldn't get a word in to dispel that fact from her mind. "And I can go to school here."

Lance sighed and shook his head. "I have to call this in. I'm going to leave it up to you, Jackson, if you want to be responsible for taking her home."

"I'll take her home." He didn't look at the woman gasping in disbelief or the kid shedding tears that dripped down her cheeks. "Next weekend. I have to make a trip to Oklahoma City with a bull calf I've sold. I can take her then."

"Keep trying to make contact with her mom. And you might want to contact a lawyer to see what your legal rights are."

"I'll do that."

Lance put the pen back in this pocket. "Jackson, don't get me in trouble with the sheriff. I'm just doing my job and I can't afford to lose my career over this."

Jackson leaned forward and shook the other man's hand. "I'll walk you to the door."

Lance pointed a finger in Jade's direction. "Running away is serious. I could call a juvenile officer. If my boss tells me to, I'll have no choice. And let me warn you, if you're thinking of running again, don't. It's December. It's cold. There are people out there who would hurt you. You're just lucky that you ended up here, with one of the best families in the state. Think about that."

"I will." Jade's eyes overflowed again.

"Take it easy on her, Lance." Jackson growled the words as they walked out of the kitchen.

"I'd love to, Jackson. But I want her to know how dangerous this is. Some kids get in the habit of running and they never stop. They end up in serious trouble, sometimes in permanent custody of the state. I don't want that to happen to her."

"You're right, but she's scared enough."

"So, you have a kid."

Jackson shrugged. If he gave up too much information, Lance would probably haul Jade in. A simple shrug and let it go, that had to be his answer for now.

He couldn't let Jade go, not now, knowing her story. That Cooper DNA was catching up with him. Take in strays and fix people. His parents had a dozen kids and more foster children because of that trait.

After watching Lance's patrol car drive away, Jackson walked back in the house. Jade and Madeline were waiting in the living room. He glanced at his watch. "We should probably eat lunch."

Madeline looked at her watch. "I need to go. I have practice."

"Okay, gotcha. What about your tree?" Jackson smiled at Jade. Her eyes and nose were red.

"I can put it up later. Jade…"

"Can stay with me. We'll cook dinner and have a nice meal waiting for you when you get home." Jackson stuttered over the words. "I mean, when you get back."

He felt itchy all over. His life didn't include a woman coming home and a kid hanging stockings on the fireplace mantel. It wasn't even a real, wood-burning fireplace.

"You don't have to do that." Madeline slipped into her coat. When she struggled to find the left sleeve, he pulled it out for her and held it as she slid her arm through.

She looked up, soft eyes and a soft smile. She smelled like hot cocoa and vanilla. He inhaled and stepped close, but then he backed off, remembering. But he couldn't let it go, not completely. He brushed a hand through her hair, pulling it loose from the collar of her coat, letting his fingers linger in the silken strands.

He took a deep breath and stepped away from her. "We'll see you later."

She nodded and hurried out the door.

Behind him Jade laughed. "I thought you were like some Casanova guy that knew all about women."

"I am and…" He grimaced. "I'm not. You know what, go clean up the kitchen."

He needed to get his act together, as his dad used to say. He needed to get his head on straight and think smart. His dad had said that too many times in his life. It had started when he dated Julia Hart. Two years older than him, and someone his mother didn't want him seen with. Julia hadn't lasted two weeks. His dad had made sure of that.

Jackson shook his head, remembering. And realizing his dad had been right most of the time.

Sometimes, though, a guy had to take a chance. He walked into the kitchen where Jade was busy putting away the dishes.

"I have an idea."

"I love ideas." She wiped at the few stray tears that rolled down her cheeks. "What is it?"

He didn't shake his head at the realization that she was just a kid, and she didn't really have anyone. But the thought hit him, broadsided him. A kid should always have someone.

Madeline had been a kid who needed someone. Probably still needed someone.

"It's a surprise for Madeline and you can help me."

Jade's eyes lit up and he only hoped that Madeline would be nearly as excited by his plan.

Chapter Seven

What Madeline loved most about Dawson was that everyone knew everyone else. What she loved least was that everyone knew everyone else's business. As she walked through the Dawson Community Center, formerly Back Street Church, she got the feeling that everyone knew. Or maybe they only thought they knew something.

She slipped past a group of teenagers who were preparing to be citizens of Bethlehem. She had a role as shepherdess, one of the few who were overwhelmed by the presence of angels in the sky on that first Christmas morning. She didn't see it as a lowly role, but as one of the most important.

It symbolized something to her, that the angels appeared to mere shepherds. Not to kings, to the wealthy or religious, but to poor shepherds watching their flocks by night. Thinking about it made her heart rush with love for the God who had loved her that much.

She hurried down the steps to the basement of the community center. Beth Hightree looked up when Madeline walked into the dressing room. Newly married,

Beth smiled with a certain glow. She held out a robe. "There's my last shepherd."

"Sorry, I meant to be here earlier." Madeline took the robe.

"I'm sure you did. Tell Jackson you have to be here early tomorrow."

"I don't know…" Madeline stopped mid-denial and shook her head. "Beth, I…"

She didn't have a clue what to say. How in the world did these people spread information so quickly?

"You don't have to explain. He's cute. He's single. You're cute and single."

"It isn't like that."

What was it like? It was a shared secret. It was about helping a neighbor who, until yesterday, hadn't even been a friend. She looked up, making uneasy eye contact with Beth.

She wouldn't lie to her. She wouldn't lie to anyone, but Beth was more than a friend. Beth, Jenna McKenzie and Madeline had formed a support group in the last year. Each had gone through a difficult situation and survived. As survivors they knew being strong meant holding on to each other and lifting each other up. Staying strong.

Beth had survived an abusive marriage.

Jenna had survived injuries suffered in Iraq.

Madeline had survived her abusive nightmare of a childhood.

They had done more than survived. They had escaped. They had overcome. They were still overcoming.

"Madeline?"

She looked up, smiling at Beth. "It isn't what you

think. I can't share what Jackson is going through. But I can tell you that I'm fine."

"Really?"

The two sat down on a little bench. Madeline held on to the rough cotton robe she still needed to change into.

"It's crazy, really. I've spent my life living in my little shell, protecting myself."

"And Jackson Cooper is cracking the shell?" Beth smiled big, her brown eyes sparkling with humor.

"No, I mean, I can't even call him a friend. I guess he's just a surprise. He's also a nice person."

Beth laughed at that. "Yes, he's a nice person. He's a flirt. He's dated more women than most of the Cooper men put together. But he's nice. He's actually sweet. And he's the last person you need to open yourself up to."

"Right. You're right." She stood and slipped the robe over her head. It hung to the floor and then some. "I think it's too long."

"I have a feeling you got the wrong robe. I saw Johnny Scott leave here in a robe about two feet too short."

"We can trade next time."

Beth handed her a long piece of rope. "Here's a belt. We can blouse it out over this and maybe you won't trip on your way up the stairs."

"That works for me." She wrapped the rope around her waist twice and then pulled to blouse the top of the robe. "Beth, I'm not going to get hurt. I'm just helping Jackson with something."

Beth nodded and reached for a box of safety pins. "I know, Madeline. The whole town knows."

Great. "There aren't any secrets in this town, are there?"

"Nope. Well, a few, but usually they get found out eventually."

Beth's words were innocent, teasing, but Madeline's mind went elsewhere, thinking about how things might change if everyone knew her secret.

"Madeline, are you okay?"

She nodded because words wouldn't come. Her throat tightened with emotion and she turned away. A hand touched her shoulder.

"Madeline, you have friends here who love you."

"I know." She hurried out of the room and up the stairs.

She knew she had friends who loved her. But suddenly she wanted more. Suddenly she wanted what she'd never wanted before. She wanted to be loved forever by a man who would walk next to her and never let her down. She wanted a man who could hear her story and not run or make her feel as if she'd done something wrong.

She didn't know if such a person existed. She remembered being little and looking up at a man she'd called Father, only to find he couldn't be trusted at all. He'd bought her ice cream and pretty dresses, and he'd taken her to the movies.

He'd taken everything from her and left her with nothing but nightmares, guilt and a heart that had closed itself off to the idea of ever being loved.

She walked outside, into bright sunlight, through the crowds of people who considered her a friend and neighbor. God had changed her life in the last few years. He'd brought her here. He'd taught her lessons about love and forgiveness.

Now it seemed as if she might be on the brink of learning another lesson, about God and about herself.

Someone touched her arm. She turned and smiled at Dixie Gordon. "Shepherds are over here. And it looks like you might have the wrong robe!"

"I think I might." As she followed Dixie her thoughts turned to Jade and Jackson, making it hard to concentrate on being a shepherd.

Out of the blue it hit her, she wanted to go home. She wanted time alone to think. She shook her head as she tripped over the robe. She wanted to be with Jade and Jackson, doing whatever it was they were doing.

She looked up, wondering how God could ask her to put her heart on the line this way. Of course she wanted to trust. But this felt like jumping into quicksand, knowing full well what it was before she jumped.

Who would do that?

The puppies barked and chased each other in the fenced-in yard. Jackson watched Jade run with them, then sit to let them crawl on her lap and lick her face. They were sable and black balls of fluff, wagging tails and sharp eyes.

Adam McKenzie shook his head and didn't say anything.

"I want a male." Jackson leaned on the fence. "They're nice-looking pups."

"Best German shepherd puppies in the state." Adam glanced his way before settling his attention back on Jade and the mother dog who had crawled up next to her for attention. "Not a mean bone in that mama dog's body. I found a male that was a good match."

"So a great pet as well as a great guard dog?"

Adam nodded. "Sure, they'll protect you. Why do you need a guard dog?"

"It isn't for me. It's for Madeline Patton."

"Oh, okay."

The tone said it all. Jackson waited for Adam to say more but Adam had turned his attention back to the girl inside the fence and the puppies. Jade picked up a puppy and it wriggled close to her, giving her face a crazy bath. She laughed and then rolled on the cold ground with the dog. "This one."

He nodded in agreement. Definitely that one. He still wanted to know what Adam McKenzie wasn't saying about him buying a dog for Madeline. What did he want Adam to do, talk him out of it? Tell him to back off before he got hooked into something he couldn't get out of.

Or better yet, tell him not to hurt her. That thought had run through his mind more times in two days than he could count.

Two days, and here he was buying a dog and remodeling her house. Yeah, big words telling Wyatt Johnson that Rachel would get under his skin. Big words, buddy.

"Talking to yourself?" Adam turned, a big grin on his face. Adam, ex-pro-football player, could squish him like a gnat.

"Not at all. We'll take that one."

Adam opened the gate for Jade to exit with the puppy.

"Fine by me, but he's a she."

Jade looked up, eyes big, pleading. But she didn't say anything. He'd learned something about her. She was pretty used to disappointment. When he'd announced that he'd have to take her home at the end of the week, she'd accepted with a quiet dignity unusual for a thirteen-year-old kid. She'd accepted it the way kids accepted when they were not ever getting what they wanted.

A home and a family shouldn't be one of the things a kid had to wish for. A kid shouldn't have to accept going back to abuse. And every time he thought about a hurting child, he shouldn't also connect dots to Madeline Patton.

He let out a long sigh and shook his head. His life was no longer his own. Not one but two females were getting under his skin.

"A girl puppy is fine." He touched the spiky, wet nose of the shepherd pup. "What do we call her?"

Jade held the puppy up, looking her in the face. "Angel."

"Angel?" He grimaced and shook his head. He should have known better than to let her name the dog. "Sure, why not. She's a guardian angel."

"Exactly." Jade pulled the puppy close again.

"How much?" Jackson pulled out his checkbook and Adam shook his head. "Adam, I'm buying the dog."

"Consider it a Christmas gift."

"I can't do that. I tell you what, I'll write you a check for Camp Hope."

"That's a deal." Adam took the check and slid it into his shirt pocket. "Have fun with that dog, Jade."

She smiled. "I will. But I have to go home next week. This is just a vacation."

A vacation from reality. Jackson put a hand on her shoulder and guided her back to the truck. *Thanks for putting a knife in my heart, kid.*

"Jade, you and I have to do something on Monday." He opened the truck door for her and she looked up.

"What's that?"

"We're going to the doctor for a test. We need to make sure we know what's going on so we know how to fight."

"How to fight?"

"Yeah, for you to be able to stay here, we have to have proof that you're my daughter." Heat climbed up his cheeks.

Jade climbed into the truck. "Sure, okay. But I am your daughter."

Yeah, he kind of wished she was. When the test came back with the results he knew they'd get, what then? What happened to Jade when she learned the truth?

When he pulled into Madeline's drive, Jade and the puppy were sleeping in the passenger side of the truck. Wake them up or leave them? He decided to let them sleep. He could get his ladder set up, find the electric box and get his work done before Madeline got back.

In a perfect world.

As he set the ladder up, the truck door opened and the twin tornadoes scrambled out. The dog ran to the corner of the yard. Jade chased after her. Jackson climbed the ladder, smiling as he listened to Jade talk to Angel. The puppy yapped and ran in circles.

He'd bought motion lights for the front porch and the back. When Madeline came home, she'd have security lights that came on with any motion. Maybe this way she could sleep at night without being afraid.

It didn't feel great, climbing the ladder. But it felt better than a few days ago. He reached for the old light, slipping it off the bracket and unscrewing the wire nuts that held the light to the light box. He wasn't an electrician, but he knew enough to hang a light.

In the yard Jade laughed and the puppy barked, yipping as the two of them raced around a tree. Every kid should have a dog. He let out a sigh, then froze as the ladder wobbled.

He looked down, the puppy stood on her hind legs, front legs on the first wrung of the ladder.

"Jade, could you get the dog?" He held the new light up to the wiring and twisted the correct wires together. He needed to connect them with the wire nut and then do the other set of wires.

Jade raced across the lawn to grab the puppy. "Sorry."

He let out a long breath and worked the other two wires together. "No problem."

The light fit into the box and he used the old screws to attach it. In a minute he'd flip the switch and make sure it worked.

The ladder wobbled again. He glanced down. That dog meant to kill him. He held tight and whistled to get Jade's attention. She'd gotten distracted, pulling Christmas lights out of the box he'd bought. She wanted Christmas lights on the front of Madeline's house.

The dog ran to the other side of the ladder. A ten-pound puppy shouldn't be able to push a ladder over. Jackson reassured himself with that bit of reality.

He grabbed the old light off the rafter of the front porch roof and slid the tools into his tool belt. He didn't want to make a scene, but he wasn't crazy about heights. A car came down the road and he knew Madeline would be home soon. It might be her now, catching him in the process of surprising her.

It wasn't.

"Here are the Christmas lights." Jade held them up, a strand of new lights.

"Sure, okay. Find the middle and I'll hook them here first."

She stretched them, pushing away the puppy who thought she'd found the best chew toy in the world. Finally she handed them up, bent where she'd found the center. He hooked them over a planter hook already in place.

Finished, he climbed down, more than a little relieved to be back on the ground. Good, solid earth. He stretched to relieve the tension in the middle of his back.

"You look a little weird," Jade announced as he moved the ladder to the end of the porch. "You okay?"

"Of course I am." He climbed the ladder and pulled the hammer from the tool belt around his waist. He pulled a nail out and made a makeshift hook for the end of the lights.

"Perfect. But hurry, she might be here in a few minutes."

"I'm hurrying. Is there even a place to plug these in?"

"Yeah, over by the door. You'll need an extension cord."

"Gotcha." He moved the ladder to the other end of the porch. The ground didn't look too level and the ladder wobbled as he climbed.

"Uh, be careful."

"You think? I'm recovering from cracked ribs and a bruised kidney. If I go down, kid, I'm taking you with me."

She laughed and he shook his head. "No respect for old people," he grumbled.

"You're not that old."

"Thanks, I think." He hammered a nail into the

wood trim of the porch roof. "There we go. She has a security light and Christmas lights."

"Isn't she too old to be afraid of the dark?" Jade moved close to the ladder.

"People are afraid of a lot of things, Jade."

"Yeah, I guess." She shook the ladder and he screamed. "Chicken."

"I'm going to get you, good."

She ran, laughing. The yapping puppy went with her. He saw another car. He turned and waved as Madeline came up the drive. Before he could make adjustments, the ladder swayed. He leaned, trying to push it back the right way. Slowly it fell backward, taking him with it.

Jade screamed. Madeline's car door slammed and she yelled.

As if he could answer as he jumped. He landed on his feet a short distance back from the ladder that crashed to the ground.

Madeline got to him before the dog. "Are you okay?"

He nodded because he couldn't really get the words out yet. These two women were determined to make him look like a weak little girl. He brushed a hand through his hair and inhaled sharply.

"Phew, that was close."

"You think?" Jade snickered and he reached for her. She moved quickly and got away.

Madeline looked up at her porch and then at him. "You put up Christmas lights."

"One better. You now have motion lights. Well, one motion light. I still have to put up the one for your back stoop."

"Jackson, you don't have to. I'm fine."

"You'll be able to sleep with the lights off." He didn't stay to discuss it with her. He picked up the ladder and headed around the side of the house, moving a little slower.

She appeared as he set up the ladder and pulled the second light out of the box. "You didn't have to do this."

"I know I didn't. I'm being a good neighbor. I should have thought of it sooner."

She stared at him, big eyes searching his face, questioning him. Probably questioning his motives, he guessed.

"Why? Why would you think of it sooner? For all you know I'm a night owl, an insomniac, addicted to computer games and coffee."

"You drink tea. Probably herbal. And you live out here by yourself."

It didn't sit right, knowing her story and her not knowing that he knew. He'd have to tell her. But how did he tell her, basically a stranger, that he knew her secrets?

"Jackson, whose puppy is that?"

He climbed the ladder and pretended to busy himself removing the old light, but he looked down at the woman standing close, holding the ladder. She didn't smile when she looked up. She didn't look away, either. He thought she had the sweetest face he'd ever seen. Pretty. She was definitely pretty. And he hadn't noticed till now because she hid behind those sweaters and big glasses.

"The puppy is yours, too. It's easier to be in the dark if you're not alone."

"I can't take a gift like that."

He hooked up the new light and twisted the wire nuts. "Yeah, you can. I've dragged you into my life and you've not asked for a thing in return. I wanted to do this for you."

"It wasn't necessary. I was helping a neighbor."

"That's what I'm doing." He climbed down. "And if you want to flip your breaker, we'll see if this works."

She nodded once and walked away. He watched her go, and he couldn't believe how much he wanted to go after her. But he stood his ground because he'd already warned himself that he wouldn't hurt her. She wasn't a woman he could casually date and then walk away from.

She had too much at stake. Too much to lose.

Madeline flipped the switch and stepped back outside to see if the light worked. Jackson stood nearby, looking up at the unlit light. He walked past and it flickered and came on. He stood beneath it in the gray light of early evening. She couldn't look away.

Jackson Cooper probably topped the list of eligible bachelors in Oklahoma. And he had just installed lights for her to sleep more securely at night. He stood in her yard, a cowboy in faded jeans and a dark blue flannel shirt. His blond hair spiked a little when he took off his hat. His slow, easy smile revealed a dimple in his chin.

Years ago she'd realized she could look at a man like Jackson and feel nothing. Which was better than the fight-or-flight instinct of her childhood. But feeling nothing had felt hollow.

Hollow but safe.

Jackson made her feel safe. But he wasn't. He could break her heart.

Because he made her feel.

"It works." He walked toward her, slow and easy, casual but she saw his grimace of pain.

"It does. Thank you."

Jade rounded the corner of the house, the puppy at

her heels. "Hey, the lights on the porch work. Come and see."

Jackson reached for her hand. Madeline drew in a breath as his fingers clasped with hers and she allowed him to lead her around to the front of her house.

"Well, look at that, you have Christmas." He tugged her close, sliding her hand with his into the pocket of her heavy coat. His fingers curled around hers, around her emotions, her heart.

She needed space. She needed to breathe deep and clear her head. She moved a step away, focusing on the glittery lights that ran along her porch roof. It took a moment for her world to settle, for her thoughts to settle. The man standing next to her had done this. For her.

A sneaky thought poked at her, asking her why he'd done this. What did he want? She brushed the suspicions aside. Jackson Cooper had done something nice for her. *Let it go.*

"Thank you." She stepped closer to the house. The floodlight he'd installed came on, taking her by surprise, making her laugh. "That might be extreme."

"You'll have to get used to it, but it'll light up the yard like it's daylight out here. And remember that every possum that crosses its path will probably set it off."

"I'll remember."

She would remember this Christmas, the year that a runaway girl pulled her into Jackson's life. The year her emotions had sprung free, totally out of control.

This moment equaled sneaking a peek at wrapped presents under the tree and then trying to shove them back into the paper, to make it the way it had been before.

An impossible task.

Jackson reached down to pet the puppy, groaning with the movement. "Jade, you need to take this dog in and feed it."

The girl turned from the lights and called the dog. The puppy ran to her new best friend and she scooped her up and headed into the house. The last thing Madeline needed in her life was a puppy. Close to the last thing she needed.

Jackson smiled down at her, his face shadowed by the brim of the cowboy hat he'd placed back on his head. "I should go."

"I could cook dinner. To pay you for all the work you've done and all the muscles you pulled jumping off the ladder." Madeline should have kept her mouth closed, let him leave.

"I'm good and we stopped at the Mad Cow. Vera cooked up fried chicken and the fixings. It's in the fridge."

"Thank you again." It sounded like a broken record now. His little kindnesses were taking her life in so many new directions she didn't know what else to say. "You can stay."

Common-sense Madeline had clearly left the building, to be replaced by out-of-control Madeline, her evil twin who obviously didn't think about broken hearts and the pain of the past.

"Thanks, but I'm going to clean up my mess and go home to crash." He picked up a few tools he'd left on the porch. "I'll get the ladder if you'll put this in the back of the truck for me."

"I can do that." She took the box, carefully avoiding eye contact with probably the most gorgeous man she'd ever met.

She walked to the back of his truck and set the box in the metal toolbox behind the cab. He returned carrying the ladder, walking a little slower. He grinned as he lifted the ladder and set it in the back of the truck.

Madeline brushed back her hair and shivered in her coat as a cold wind picked up, scattering dried leaves left over from autumn across her lawn. She looked up and he had moved closer, his hazel eyes settled on her face, watching her, touching her with a look.

When his hand touched her arm she closed her eyes, waiting, telling herself not to run from this, not to run from feeling too much. His fingers touched her chin, turning her to face him.

Grounded, she was grounded. Reality, not fear. She was in her yard. The earth was beneath her. The truck was close enough to touch. A car drove by. A neighbor honked. She opened her eyes, no longer afraid. Much.

His hand moved to her cheek, sweet and easy. His fingers tangled in her hair and she looked up, wanting to know what it meant to be the woman in his arms.

When he pulled her close she froze for just an instant, then she exhaled and let go. He leaned in, soft breath and mint. The tangy scent of his cologne mixed with the winter air, a sharp breeze and wood smoke from the neighbor's fireplace. His hand slid to her waist and he held her for just a moment.

And as quick as that, he backed away, leaving her standing there in her driveway, unsure. Shaken.

He smiled and shook his head.

"Madeline, you're tempting, and self-control is not one of my strongest character traits. Some would say I have no control when it comes to beautiful women." His fingers touched her cheek, feather-soft. "But I always keep my word and I'm going to do that right now and walk away."

She backed away from him, not sure how to take this moment, this goodbye. Her heart raced and she breathed, trying to catch up. Jackson Cooper tipped his hat and got into his truck.

As she stood there trying to make sense of what had happened, he backed out of her drive and was gone. She had put her heart on the line, taken steps she'd never taken before. She'd been rejected.

Jackson Cooper, known for his many relationships, for having a constant string of women, had held her and walked away.

So what did that make her? Chopped liver?

For a long time she stood in her driveway, shivering in the cold wind and trying hard not to be hurt by his rejection. But it did hurt. Because she'd held her emotions in check for so many years and when she'd taken a step toward someone, the man had walked away.

It hurt because his daughter was in her house and she'd have to see him again tomorrow.

As she walked back into the house she told herself it didn't have to be him. He didn't have to be the man she took a chance with. She could find someone safe. Someone who wouldn't break her heart.

But she had a hard time convincing herself.

Chapter Eight

Jackson had to admit to a moment of real doubt as he walked up the steps of Dawson Community Church. Church, for the first time in… Well, he'd gone to funerals and weddings, but hadn't gone to church in ten years or more.

Except Christmas and Easter. He'd done the holidays for his mom.

Today he walked up the steps and through the door for… Himself? Jade? Or maybe for Madeline? Because last night he'd walked away from her, seconds short of a moment that he figured would have changed his life and hers in ways he couldn't take back.

His dad had warned him Madeline wasn't someone to play around with. Madeline had stories that he couldn't begin to fathom and pain that he wished he could take away. He wanted to hold on to her and promise no one would ever hurt her again. He was the last person to make that promise.

Church had already started. He walked through the double doors and into the vestibule. He stood there rethinking the impulse that had put him in church on a Sunday morning, dress boots and new jeans, a button-up shirt he'd actually ironed. He took off the black cowboy hat he'd shoved on his head as he got out of the truck and held it in his hand.

Someone stepped forward, reaching for his hand. Ryder Johnson. Not much more than a year ago Ryder had been single and he'd planned on staying that way. Now he had a wife and twin baby girls.

"Jackson, good to see you," Ryder whispered as he pulled him into a comfortable man hug and slapped him on the back. And then Ryder ruined things by whispering, "And look, the roof is still in one piece."

"Yeah, thanks." Jackson spotted a seat on the back pew. The piano played and the choir sang "I'll Fly Away."

"It really is good to have you here."

"Good to be here." Jackson sat down and Ryder went back to his seat next to his wife, Andie.

Jackson settled into the seat by himself in an empty pew. A few people looked back, wondering. His Gram sat near the front next to his dad. Her smile split her face and she nodded and looked up, thinking God had, at long last, answered prayers for the grandson gone astray.

He closed his eyes as the choir took their seats and Jenna McKenzie sang a solo. He felt someone move close, sit next to him. A body brushed past him. He opened his eyes and smiled at Jade, who'd taken her place to his left. And Madeline to his right.

Oh yeah, this wouldn't be a rumor starter. And a match on dry wood wouldn't start a fire. Right! By the end of the day everyone in town would be talking and they'd have a hard time deciding what to discuss first. Jackson Cooper had gone to church and the roof hadn't caved. Madeline and a girl that looked a lot like him had sat next to him in church. So much for slipping in unnoticed.

"You're here." Jade grabbed his hand. She peeked past him to Madeline. "I told you."

"Shhh," Madeline warned. "We're in church."

Jade nodded but she held on to his hand.

Somehow he managed to focus on the sermon about killing giants with faith. A decent twist on a story he'd heard all his life. Giants. He'd had a few that he'd faced in his life. He couldn't really say what had pushed him out of church. Maybe a lifetime of being told to get up, to clean up, to stop acting up? Maybe being busy, being gone on Sundays? Maybe shame for the things he'd done that he knew would make his mother blush and probably make God none too happy?

Today didn't really push him to the top of any spiritual mountains. Everyone in town knew him for what he was. Today they would think he was a dad. The kid sitting next to him, holding on to his hand like he was some kind of hero, thought he was her dad.

Maybe they'd think he was involved with everyone's favorite teacher. He had to admit, he didn't dislike the notion of people thinking he'd managed to snag someone who smelled like a spring morning.

Her arm touched his.

"Lunch at the Cooper Ranch after church," he whispered close to her ear.

She shivered and he moved his arm, settling it on the back of the pew behind her. Lunch with the family, a Sunday tradition. Even when he didn't go to church he still had lunch with the family. Most of the time.

But he never took a woman with him. The word *date* slipped into his mind. He'd never taken a date to Sunday lunch. That hadn't seemed right. Not attending

Holiday Blessing

ough without him adding a

 on the front of the church
his heart. It happened when
xt to his dad. Travis sat next
ky and his wife and kids.
n there, but he'd joined the
 out to Afghanistan.
with bank business, didn't

n Grove. She liked anonym-

uty at the hospital.
lls in Texas, and Gage was

g these days, and usually it
 family.
ies and places to be.
re sooner. If not for himself,
her face when she turned at
ve that thought home. Yeah,
d, for himself, but his mom
t him, with tears in her eyes.
er everyone stood, people
h sense to know that most
way. Jackson in church on a
ay? They'd all be wondering

clasped his hand and shot a
de. "You coming out to the

. "You bringing your little

Jackson squeezed the hand that still held his. "Travis, don't make me have to take you out back."

Travis laughed and pulled away, a good-natured pup who needed a serious thump on the head. "Nothing wrong with settling down, brother. The three of you look kind of nice together."

Jackson reached but Travis moved a little quicker these days.

And then his parents stepped close. This had gone from a decent idea to one huge complication. Jade was in his mother's arms and his mom stared at him, eyes wide, lots of questions and answers.

Sooner or later he would have to talk to Jade, explain things to her. But looking at her in the middle of his big family, watching her smile and laugh, he knew it wouldn't be easy and it would break her heart. He could give the kid Christmas with his family. That's what she wanted, a family.

"Are you coming out to the house for lunch?" His mom still held on to Jade and with her free hand she reached for Madeline, pulling her close. And they were all looking at him.

Yeah, he'd planned on lunch with his family. Now that plan seemed to include the two females who were doing a lot to complicate his, up to now, uncomplicated life. Yesterday it had felt good to do something nice for Madeline. It had felt pretty decent to spend an afternoon with Jade.

But taking them home to his family felt a little... He pulled at the collar of his shirt and wished it was not quite so hot.

"Jackson?" His dad shot him a look.

"Of course we're coming out for lunch." He avoided

looking at Madeline but he couldn't miss the very pleased smile on his mother's face.

Sandwiched on the truck seat between Jade and Jackson, Madeline tried to make herself smaller. She sat up straight and kept her shoulders in. The truck turned and she slid a little toward Jackson in his new jeans, his dark cowboy hat covering blond hair that managed to look a little messy and made him a whole lot cute.

For the first time in her life, she felt young. She felt like a sixteen-year-old in a pickup on a Saturday night. It felt good. And frightening.

"Nervous?" Jackson smiled, eyes crinkling at the corners, and then shifted his attention back to the road. He reached to turn up the radio and an old Randy Travis song filled the cab of the truck. *Forever and ever, Amen.*

She'd never thought about loving someone forever. She'd always thought that being single meant being safe from being hurt. Safe now seemed to be a thing of the past.

"Of course not. Why would I be nervous?"

He laughed loud. "You and I both know that this isn't a simple lunch. The minute you sat down next to me, everyone in Dawson had us paired up and started wondering when we'd be announcing the big day."

She choked a little because she hadn't expected him to put it so bluntly. "Thanks."

His left hand firmly on the wheel, he moved his right arm and slipped it around her shoulder. His fingers tweaked her sleeve, and her arm buzzed beneath his touch.

"It's okay, Maddie, we'll get through this and in a

week or two, people will realize you were the person rescuing me and Jade."

Why didn't that make her feel any better? Because he'd just let her know, in a sweet way, that she wasn't anything more than the person helping him out? Why did it suddenly, painfully, matter?

They pulled up the driveway that led to the main house of the Cooper ranch, the Circle C. Cooper Creek flowed through the field and circled back through the stand of trees farther on. The house, a big, brick, Georgian place, sat back from the main road. Trees lined the driveway.

The Coopers were everything a family should be. The Coopers were everything she'd ever wanted. Probably everything Jade had ever wanted. Not that they didn't have problems, but when they did, they drew together and held on to each other.

She'd never really had a family. Hers had been a group of people and it had never been safe or nurturing. Foster care had been a respite for a few years but she'd been too closed off at that time to get attached to her foster parents. She'd kept in touch for a few years but she'd finally stopped writing.

"They don't bite." Jackson leaned close as he pulled to a stop behind another car. Lucky's family piled out of an SUV. Jackson's hand rubbed her arm and he pulled her close for a brief instant.

"I know they don't." But her heart pounded hard, achingly hard. Not because of the prospect of lunch with the Coopers, but because Jackson's arm around her held her tight.

He held her tight and she wasn't afraid, not of him.

"You okay?"

"I'm good." Not good.

Her heart crumbled a little with the knowledge that it was this man who made her feel safe. It shouldn't be him. It didn't make sense that safety and fear should tangle together in her heart, pushing against each other.

Jade had already jumped out of the truck. Jackson reached for his door and settled one last look on her before pushing it open. "Time to face the music, Maddie."

"So sweetly put." She ignored the hand he held out. "I should have gone home. You could have spent this day with Jade and your family."

"My mother would have taken a switch to me if you hadn't come along."

"I doubt that."

He laughed and pulled her close. "Darlin', you have no idea. My mom is probably thinking you're one of the answers to her prayers. All our lives she's prayed for God to send the perfect person into our lives at the perfect moment. And she has no doubt that God will honor that prayer."

"But I'm not…"

"You won't be able to convince her of that." He leaned close, and she wondered if he meant to kiss her. He didn't. He flicked her chin with his finger and stepped away.

She obviously brought this new self-control out in him. *Way to go, Madeline.* For the first time she wanted to be held and for the first time in his life, Jackson Cooper had self-control.

Madeline took a deep breath and stood a little straighter. Time to face the music. She managed a smile and to not melt when Jackson held her hand and walked her up the steps of the big house, straight into the circle of trust that was the Coopers.

Jade didn't seem to have a problem. She stood in the middle of Jackson's very overwhelming family and allowed them to pull her in.

"What's for lunch, Mom?" Jackson's thumb brushed the top of Madeline's hand and he didn't let go.

Angie Cooper turned, smiling big, reaching for Madeline and forcing Jackson to let go. Madeline loved Angie Cooper. She was gracious, dignified and always kind.

"Madeline, thank you so much for helping Jackson with this…situation."

"It hasn't been a problem."

Angie's smile softened as did her expression. "Of course it hasn't. But it means so much to us."

Coopers were everywhere. They were laughing and talking, teasing each other. Angie Cooper continued to talk, not bothered at all by the constant commotion around her. Her family. Jackson's family.

Madeline nodded in answer to Angie's questions. In the blink of an eye Jackson stood next to her. She smiled up at him, pretending to be strong, because she'd pretended for a long time. But in the middle of this family she felt so much like a fraud, because she'd never had a family, not a real one.

She was strong. She'd spent the last fifteen years telling herself she was a survivor, not a victim. But survivors still had to deal with the past, with fear, with leftover anger and resentment.

With baggage that didn't unpack itself.

She'd done a lot of baggage unpacking. There were a few little things she still carried around with her, she knew that. But eventually she knew she'd let it all go. She'd trust enough to let it go.

She brushed a hand across her cheeks to wipe away

stray tears that had trickled out before she could get control of her emotions.

"Let's walk." Jackson took her by the hand. "Mom, we'll be right in to help set the table."

Angie Cooper shot her son a narrow-eyed look. "Jackson."

"Five minutes." He winked at his mom.

Madeline thought about telling him no. But for Jackson, his charm seemed to come naturally. He could wink at his mom, smile and they all went along with his plans. At that moment she had no choice but to go with him. She either went or she fell apart in front of his family.

Somehow he knew that she needed a minute to gather herself. Later she would thank him for that little bit of intuition. Later she might even wonder how he knew her so well.

Hand in hand they walked out the front door, down the steps and across the lawn. Neither of them spoke, which was good. What would she say when they did speak? Sorry for being so ridiculous?

At a small gazebo at the edge of the lawn they finally stopped. Jackson smiled down at her, a gentle smile. No wink. No flirty grin. "I wanted to make sure you're okay. I thought a little fresh air might help."

She nodded, unsure. "I'm fine, really I am."

He stood in front of her, and she felt as if he saw everything about her. Including the things she didn't want him to see. He touched her cheek. "You're sure? Because I recognize that 'need to escape this family' look."

"I'm sure." She laughed a little because she had been thinking exactly that.

Was that part of Jackson's charm? He could read

people and it made a woman think that he really cared, really understood? Of course that was it, and for that reason alone she should back away.

He shouldn't be the man she wanted to kiss. She moved closer and his brows arched. His hand moved from hers. He slid it around her back and held her close. But he didn't kiss her.

Okay, fine, she would make the first move. She could do this, even if she fainted in the process. She didn't plan on living her life in a box, afraid to feel. Braver than she'd ever been in her life, she stood on her tiptoes and rested a hand on his shoulder. Jackson whispered her name as he bent and drew her close. Telling herself she wouldn't regret it, she touched her lips to his, closing her eyes to the landslide of feelings that slammed her heart.

"Madeline." He pulled back first.

"I'm sorry." She didn't know what else to say. "I can't believe I did that."

"You don't have to apologize." He winked—a little of the old Jackson obviously still existed.

She had kissed Jackson Cooper and he had pulled away. Now she had to go back in the house with him, sit at the table with him, and pretend it didn't hurt to be rejected, to be the woman that Jackson Cooper could resist.

She blamed herself. She'd taken a single moment and turned it into something it hadn't been, ever. He had done a few sweet things for her and she'd obviously taken it wrong. Last night she'd thought he would kiss her and he hadn't. She should have learned then that he wasn't interested.

As she hurried up the steps he called her name. She didn't turn back. She wouldn't. She'd been humiliated enough. For years she'd been praying that God would help her move past her fear. This probably hadn't been His plan.

The front door of the house opened. Heather Cooper, blonde, petite, pretty, smiled. "Madeline, Mom told me you were here today. She said to find you and Jackson."

Heather peeked around her. "There he is." And then her attention refocused on Madeline, and Madeline wanted to melt into the concrete of the front porch. "Are you okay? What did he do?"

Nervousness turned to hysteria. Madeline giggled and then laughed. She turned to watch Jackson walk up the steps, still the gentleman, shrugging and saying nothing.

"Nothing happened." Madeline wouldn't let him take the fall for her mistake. "Nothing at all."

She hurried inside the house and left Jackson with his sister. Nothing at all had happened. Nothing would ever happen. Jackson had given her the space she needed to come to her senses.

He had rejected her. That knowledge settled in her heart where it felt heavy and cold. And she had to go in to lunch with him, sit across the table from him and avoid looking his way.

Which she could do because she'd always avoided him. She needed to do that for a little longer, and then she would put distance between them. Jade could stay with his family. Madeline could go back to her life. Thanks to Jackson, she could walk away without regret.

At the moment, thanking him was the last thing she wanted to do.

Chapter Nine

After a pretty miserable lunch, Jackson loaded Madeline and Jade back into his truck and drove them to the church where they'd left Madeline's car a few hours earlier. A five-minute ride felt like five hours with neither of the women in his truck speaking. The younger one seemed to be talked out—finally.

The older one looked hurt and wounded. Exactly what he hadn't wanted to happen. He'd been doing his best to protect her and she'd messed that up royally.

Jackson pulled his truck into the church parking lot, stopping next to Madeline's sedan. Jade dozed in the seat next to him. Madeline had managed to sit near the door this time. He had thought long and hard about that kiss, about the hurt look on her face when she ran away.

He couldn't let her go home thinking this was about her. The woman who hid behind big sweaters and glasses needed to understand that he hadn't rejected her because of her.

But when would he tell her, and what would he say? Nothing for now, not in front of Jade. Not in the church parking lot when he would be driving home and she'd go back to her house.

"Jade, climb on in Madeline's car. I'll follow you back to your house." He nudged the sleeping teenager.

"We'll be fine." Madeline opened the truck door. "I'll bring Jade to your house in the morning before I go to work."

"I know I don't have to follow you, but I'm going to. We need to talk."

Madeline moved for Jade to get out of the truck. "We don't need to talk. Really, I don't want to talk. I think we've said it all."

"We actually haven't said a word and I want to explain."

"No, thank you." She got out and closed the door.

Jackson watched as she rummaged through her purse for her keys. She had reverted to glasses today and a big brown sweater with a denim skirt. He shook his head as she fumbled, dropped her purse and then opened the car door and tossed it in the back seat. Angry gestures. Mad at him or mad at herself?

After she drove away Jackson sat there in the parking lot, thinking about a lot of stuff, most of which didn't make sense. He didn't need this. His life was fine. He had his ranch. He had his family and friends.

This church that had always been in his life, he even had that, when he wanted.

When he wanted? On his schedule, his time?

Okay, he got that God might not like that idea. So this was all some "jerk you up by the seat of your pants" faith plan? He remembered the chorus of an old hymn his grandmother loved.

No turning back, no turning back.

He could argue all day that he kind of liked the old Jackson, the old life, but God was sending a pretty clear

HOW TO VALIDATE YOUR
EDITOR'S FREE GIFTS!
"THANK YOU"

1. Peel off the FREE GIFTS SEAL from the front cover. Place it in the space provided at right. This automatically entitles you to receive two free books and two exciting surprise gifts.

2. Send back this card and you'll get 2 Love Inspired® books. These books have a combined cover price of $11.50 for the regular-print and $13.00 for the larger-print in the U.S. and $13.50 for the regular-print or $15.00 for the larger-print in Canada, but they are yours to keep absolutely FREE!

3. There's no catch. You're under no obligation to buy anything. We charge nothing—ZERO—for your first shipment. And you don't have to make any minimum number of purchases—not even one!

4. We call this line Love Inspired because every month you'll receive books that are filled with joy, faith and traditional values. The stories will lift your spirit and warm your heart! You'll like the convenience of getting them delivered to your home well before they are in stores. And you'll love our discount prices, too!

5. We hope that after receiving your free books you'll want to remain a subscriber. But the choice is yours—to continue or cancel, anytime at all! So why not take us up on our invitation, with no risk of any kind. You'll be glad you did!

6. And remember...just for validating your Editor's Free Gifts Offer, we'll send you 2 books and 2 gifts, *ABSOLUTELY FREE!*

YOURS FREE!

We'll send you two fabulous surprise gifts (worth about $10) absolutely FREE, simply for accepting our no-risk offer!

The Editor's "Thank You" Free Gifts Include:

- Two inspirational romance books
- Two exciting surprise gifts

YES!

PLACE FREE GIFTS SEAL HERE

I have placed my Editor's "thank you" Free Gifts seal in the space provided above. Please send me the 2 FREE books and 2 FREE gifts for which I qualify. I understand that I am under no obligation to purchase anything further, as explained on the opposite page.

❏ I prefer the regular-print edition
105/305 IDL FJLP

❏ I prefer the larger-print edition
122/322 IDL FJLP

Please Print

FIRST NAME

LAST NAME

ADDRESS

APT.#   CITY

STATE/PROV.   ZIP/POSTAL CODE

The Reader Service—Here's How It Works:

Accepting your 2 free books and 2 free gifts (gifts valued at approximately $10.00) places you under no obligation to buy anything. You may keep the books and gifts and return the shipping statement marked "cancel." If you do not cancel, about a month later we will send you 6 additional books and bill you just $4.49 each for the regular-print edition or $4.99 each for the larger-print edition in the U.S. or $4.99 each for the regular-print edition or $5.49 each for the larger-print edition in Canada. That is a savings of at least 22% off the cover price. It's quite a bargain! Shipping and handling is just 50¢ per book in the U.S. and 75¢ per book in Canada.* You may cancel at any time, but if you choose to continue, every month we'll send you 6 more books, which you may either purchase at the discount price or return to us and cancel your subscription.

*Terms and prices subject to change without notice. Prices do not include applicable taxes. Sales tax applicable in N.Y. Canadian residents will be charged applicable taxes. Offer not valid in Quebec. All orders subject to credit approval. Credit or debit balances in a customer's account(s) may be offset by any other outstanding balance owed by or to the customer. Please allow 4 to 6 weeks for delivery. Offer available while quantities last.

▲ If offer card is missing write to: The Reader Service, P.O. Box 1867, Buffalo, NY 14240-1867 or visit www.ReaderService.com ▲

BUSINESS REPLY MAIL
FIRST-CLASS MAIL   PERMIT NO. 717   BUFFALO, NY

POSTAGE WILL BE PAID BY ADDRESSEE

THE READER SERVICE
PO BOX 1867
BUFFALO NY 14240-9952

NO POSTAGE
NECESSARY
IF MAILED
IN THE
UNITED STATES

message. No turning back. It set him back on his heels a little, and he took a long time getting back on the road.

Tomorrow he'd move forward. He'd go to his doctor in Grove.

He'd try, again, to get hold of Gloria Baker.

And he'd fix things with Madeline.

Tonight, though, he'd find a way to get his mind off the crazy twists and turns his life had taken. First he drove past Madeline's, making sure she and Jade got in the house safely. The porch light burned bright. She'd parked her car under the carport.

He turned his truck around in her driveway and headed back to town, in the direction of Back Street. He had work to do on the living nativity. Since the horse had thrown him and then Jade showed up, he'd kind of neglected his job of building Bethlehem.

The front porch light of Dawson Community Center cast a wide arc of light across the front lawn of what had once been his family church. There were a lot of memories tied to this little building. Most were pleasant, some weren't.

One that he had mixed feelings about had to do with Jeremy Hightree, his half brother. They'd grown up together, not knowing that they shared the same father. Today they were probably closer than ever. But the relationship was still strained. It took a lot for a guy like Jeremy to let go of pride and resentment. Jackson figured Jeremy had done better than he would have.

After parking he grabbed tools out of the back of his truck and walked across the lawn to the makeshift buildings. An inn, shops, and on the other side of the lawn, the manger scene. He needed to work on the inn. He strapped a tool belt around his waist and hooked the hammer into the loop.

Ioliday Blessing

re tonight?"

at Jeremy and pulled nails
uld talk. "Thought I'd get
of fallen behind on the job."
ou fell off a horse. I didn't
days."

few days, now do we?"
valked a little closer. "No,
u at church today. A little

ne advice, if you don't mind.
you were running hard and
l to do with Dawson." Jack-
looking at Jeremy. "As a
a dozer aimed at this build-

ot a point."
l a nail and lifted the board
"What would you do with-

my stepped closer and Jack-
sn't smiling. "I'm just going

a second Jackson wondered
hed. Jeremy smiled but his
evening light.
ours, you'd better not leave

ed, he bristled. Jackson felt
remy looked a little ahead
a fight. He put the hammer
from Jeremy. He got it. He
say something like that to

him. Jeremy had spent most of his life feeling like baggage that got left on the side of the road.

"I think you know me better than that." Jackson picked the hammer up again. He tapped the nail into place, and reached for another. "And you don't really know a thing about this situation."

"I know that everyone in town is talking about a kid showing up on your doorstep claiming to be yours and looking a lot like you."

"People assume a lot, don't they?"

"Maybe they do, but sometimes the facts point to the obvious answer."

Jackson pushed a tarp out of the way and pulled a piece of plywood across the opening. "I'm really not going to have this discussion with you."

Jeremy didn't budge. He didn't back down. "I guess it isn't any of my business. And I guess I'm making it my business because she's a kid and I know what it feels like to be that kid, wanting to be a part of a family."

Jackson exhaled a whole lot of frustration. He finally looked at Jeremy, shaking his head and wishing he'd gone on home. Instead he'd come here thinking he could work alone, get his thoughts together and figure out what to do.

That's what he got for thinking.

"She isn't mine."

Jeremy stared for a long minute and then looked up at the sky. When he zeroed in on Jackson, it felt pretty uncomfortable. Jackson's attention focused on a closed fist and then on the hard stare.

"Really?"

Jackson picked up another board and nailed it to the frame of what would soon be the inn that turned Mary and Joseph away. For all eternity it would be the inn that turned away a baby, the son of God, the savior.

But the story would have changed if Jesus hadn't been born in that manger, the humblest of circumstances. He might not go to church every Sunday but Jackson got that God always had a plan. Things came together for a reason.

A young girl had landed on his doorstep. For a reason?

"Jeremy, she isn't mine. I know that she looks a lot like a Cooper and my name is on the birth certificate. But I'm about one hundred percent certain she isn't mine."

"'About'?"

"I'm done with this conversation. I'm either going to finish the inn or knock you into the middle of next week. Which do you prefer, brother?"

Jeremy raised his hands and backed away. "You go right ahead and finish the inn."

"Thank you, I will." Jackson pounded another nail with Jeremy watching.

Of course he wouldn't be quiet for long. Finally he cleared his throat and stepped forward again.

"She's a cute kid and she seems pretty high on you." Jeremy cleared his throat again. "As a matter of fact, she isn't the only one who seems to really like you these days. Two women, is that a record?"

"It isn't a record and you're a piece of…"

Jeremy slapped him on the back, laughing loud. "Jackson, I'm the best thing that ever happened to you. I'm your brother."

"I don't know how you think that's a good thing."

Jeremy backed toward the door. "Well, I haven't knocked you on your can yet. And I put up with you coming over here in the evening, making noise and bellowing like an angry bull."

"I put up with you on Sundays and holidays." More than that, but he wasn't in the mood to be congenial.

"I'm going to give you a sweet little niece or nephew in about eight months."

Jackson froze, holding the board, pretty amazed. "Seriously, you and Beth?"

"We're having a baby."

"Congratulations." Jackson meant it, but today it didn't come out as easily as it once would have. Today he could only think about the little girl who wasn't his and the woman who had kissed him this afternoon, unsettling him, and changing his mind about a lot of things.

"Thanks. It's going to be a big change for us." Jeremy grinned and snorted a laugh. "At least we get to work up to it. No 'surprise, it's a teenager' for us."

"You're a laugh a minute."

"I try. Hey, it's getting late and Beth will wonder where I am. Why don't you head on home? We'll get some more work done here on Wednesday."

"Yeah, I think that's a good idea." He slipped the hammer into the tool belt and stretched, groaning when the muscles between his shoulders protested. "I think it's time to go home and put my feet up."

"Let me know if I can do anything to help." Jeremy walked out the door ahead of him.

"Yeah, I'll do that."

A few minutes later Jackson drove down the road, slowing as he got close to Madeline's driveway. Every light in the house was on. A week ago he would have gone on by, wondering about her, maybe smiling.

Tonight he pulled in, parking behind her car.

It took her a few minutes to answer the door. He knocked a little louder, rethinking the decision to stop by. The puppy barked and Jade shouted, which meant he couldn't leave now. He had to stand there, not quite sure of himself. He pushed his hat back and waited.

Who was he kidding? His mom said he'd been sure of himself since he turned three and managed to kiss Annie Butler on the cheek in the church nursery. He grinned, not that he remembered, but he liked that story. Even if Annie hadn't ever dated him.

Commotion erupted inside the house. He peeked between the curtains and saw Jade race through the hall, the dog following her. Madeline yelled that she would get it and for Jade to get in the shower.

Wow, domestic. Family. Not at all what he had been thinking about. A book on the table and a coffee cup. Pictures on the walls. The smell of wood smoke filled the air. A cat hopped up on the porch and sat looking at him, licking its paw and blinking the way cats did.

The door opened a crack. Madeline peeked, sighed and opened the door the rest of the way.

"Why are you here?"

He shrugged. "Guess I felt like we have unfinished business."

"Really? I think it's all been said. Jackson, can't you let a woman crawl off and hide without you chasing her down and making her remember that she made a fool of herself?"

He moved a little into the door. "You didn't make a fool of yourself, so that isn't why I'm here. And I'm afraid I do like to be the one who chases the woman."

"So this is because…" Her cheeks turned pink. "Because *I* kissed *you*."

"And hurt my male ego?" He smiled and then

laughed. "It isn't that at all. Why don't you invite me in for a cup of tea? It's cold out here."

And he wasn't a tea person. But he thought she probably was. He could hear water running and knew Jade would be out of the shower soon.

"Okay, tea." Madeline led the way through a house he'd been in hundreds of times in his life. His great-grandparents had lived here. His grandmother had grown up here.

Jackson took a seat at her tiny dining room table. A poinsettia graced the center. She'd put her Christmas tree in the corner of her little dining room. Jackson watched as she moved around the kitchen heating water, finding tea bags and placing cups on the counter.

After a minute he stood, because he couldn't sit and watch her. He had to stand near her, watch her expressions, her serious brown eyes. He knew her story, but he wanted to know everything about her. He wanted her to share her dreams with him. He wanted to hear her laugh.

He'd dated a lot of women who talked nonstop, whose constant stories about themselves grated on his nerves. This woman didn't talk enough.

"The other day when I was looking for information on Gloria Baker," he said, leaning against the counter. Madeline kept her back to him. She poured steaming water in the two cups. "I searched your name."

She nodded but still didn't turn to look at him. "Okay."

"I know what happened when you were a little girl."

She poured hot water in the cups and didn't look up. It took everything for him to stay in that spot, watching her, not moving toward her, not reaching for her hands that trembled, not putting an arm around her when she shivered.

He knew all the right moves. He'd spent his life studying women, figuring out how they ticked. He knew how to make them feel special. This time he didn't know. Or maybe he did. Maybe standing there, letting her pull herself together, not reaching for her was the best move.

It was just a new page in his life. A new game plan.

"Why are you telling me this?" Her voice trembled but there were no tears.

"I'm telling you to explain that I didn't pull away because of you. I pulled away because of who I am. I don't want to be another person that hurts you. And let me tell you, I'm the guy who could. I've had plenty of angry messages on my answering machine. I've dated a lot of women and most of them are no longer in my life. A few still send me Christmas cards. Thirteen years ago one of those women put my name on a birth certificate as the father of her child. I'm keeping my distance because I don't want to hurt you."

"What did you learn about me?" She turned, handing him a cup of tea before walking away. He watched her take a seat at the oak dinette.

When he'd searched her name he hadn't really expected to learn anything. He hadn't expected to learn information that would change his life. Maybe hers.

"I guess I learned everything. Or at least the facts available on the internet. But there's more to you than that story."

"It isn't something I share with many people, Jackson. It isn't a great opening line. Hi, I was born and raised in a cult. My mom worshipped a man who convinced her that all of the women owed him their little girls."

"You were a victim."

She shrugged. "It's my past. It changes how people think of you when they learn something like that. Doesn't it?"

He moved to the seat across from her, carrying the cup of steaming tea in a tiny little cup that represented the woman staring up at him with liquid brown eyes and a soft smile that trembled and faded.

"I'm sorry." What could he say? That he wanted to find that man and hurt him for what he'd done to her and countless other children. He didn't need for her to share the story of a man who used little girls as objects, dividing them amongst his disciples, marrying them off at young ages after their innocence was already stolen from them. He didn't want for her to have to tell him the story in her words. The story was on her face, in her eyes and hidden in her heart.

But she'd survived.

Her hands trembled as she sipped the tea. The cup clattered in the saucer when she set it on the table. He kept his hands on the porcelain cup of amber liquid, thinking it should make him calm, but it didn't.

"You don't have to be sorry." She smiled up at him, brave, amazing. Too good for him. "Unless you mean you're sorry for snooping."

He laughed a little, surprised by her smile, her soft laughter. "I am sorry about that. I'm sorry if anyone ever treats you differently because of what you've been through. You are more than what happened to you in that place."

"I know." She sniffled a little and reached for a napkin in the basket on the table. "I get caught feeling blessed because I escaped with fewer scars than so many of the children. And then I feel guilty because I escaped. I owe Sara everything."

"Your sister?"

Madeline nodded again. She held her cup of tea in both hands, not drinking it. He sipped his, waiting, not wanting to push.

"She took me to town. And then she disappeared. I haven't seen or heard from her since."

"Your parents?"

"I don't know who my real father is. My mother finds me and sends a Christmas or birthday card every year or so." She glanced toward the hall, toward the bathroom where water still poured from the shower.

"Your mother is out of prison?"

She nodded. "Jackson, I'm glad I can help you with Jade, but you have to understand. I've spent years trying to convince myself that it wasn't my fault."

He held the cup of tea because he wanted to hit something. Or somebody.

"I've been numb. I've been afraid. And over the years, I've been happy with my life." Her brown eyes twinkled. "Even when I sleep with the lights on."

Jackson reached for her hands. He moved them from the cup and he held them in his. "I haven't had a lot of experience with this, but I think I make a pretty good friend."

She laughed at that. And laughed some more. When Jackson started to let go of her hands, she held tight until her laughter dissolved and she had to wipe her eyes.

"What's so funny?"

She laughed again. "You, being a girl's friend. The

idea of it makes you turn a little red." She touched her neck. "From here up."

Footsteps in the hall meant they were about to have company. Laughter and the dog barking. Madeline smiled. "You have definitely unsettled my life. My neat little house is suddenly chaos, clutter and a Christmas movie come to life."

"I hope that's a good thing. I think we've both been a little unsettled this week."

"More than a little." Her eyes darted toward the door. Still no sign of Jade. "I think she's not as happy as she pretends to be."

"I think you're right about that. I think she's trying to pretend this is some great adventure."

"We can't run from life."

"No, we can't." He stood, leaving the nearly empty tea cup on the table. Maybe he was a tea person after all. "I'll see you tomorrow."

She followed him to the door. He could still hear Jade and the dog. They were probably in the spare bedroom at the back of the house. It was probably better that she didn't crash in on this conversation.

He knew Madeline's story. She still didn't know his. He thought that one was better saved for after the doctor's appointment he'd made for the next day. A DNA test and a check-up.

"Jackson, thank you." She stood on the front porch, hugging her sweater around her thin frame. The full moon captured her features, her big eyes and sweet smile.

"You're welcome." He leaned in, kissing her goodbye. An easy kiss on the cheek. "I'm getting very good at this."

Her eyes narrowed. "At what?"

er and walked down off the
nd thinking that maybe self-
thing. But she didn't need to

could give her a simple kiss
ood-night, or an easy hug. He
ake her feel safe. Friendship.
endship.
self that.

"I think you're right about
to pretend this is some great

"We can't run from life."

"No, we can't," He stood,
tea cup on the table. Maybe
all. "I'll see you tomorrow."

She followed him to the
side and the dog. They were
room at the back of the hous
that she didn't crash in on th
the lenten Medit… Joe's story
He thought that one was …
for a reception, hed made
tea and a made-up …

"Take care, thank you." She
hugging her, sweater around
moved captured her feelings,
smiled.

"You're welcome." He lea
two. An easy kiss on the chee
at this.

He was narrowed. "At w

Chapter Ten

Mondays were always hard for Madeline. The kids were fresh from the weekend, lots of energy, homework not done and attitudes definitely not in check. This Monday proved to be even more difficult. She couldn't relax and the kids were bouncing off the walls. When she left at the end of the day she wanted nothing more than a long soak in the tub and a nice, easy dinner. Maybe takeout from the Mad Cow.

But halfway home she remembered Jade. She remembered Jackson. She remembered all the ways her life had changed in the last few days. And none of it had been her doing. A few weeks ago in their Sunday school class Clint Cameron had taught how God changed our lives to make more room for Him and His plan. She hadn't really thought about it before. She'd made her own changes, such as buying a home, forcing herself to stay and not run.

God had brought other changes. She hadn't thought about Jade or Jackson in that light. She'd thought about Jade on her doorstep as a mistaken address and bad directions.

What did any of this have to do with her? Maybe

God wanted to use this situation to show her that she could open up to people. More specifically, that she could trust a man. Of all the men she should be expected to trust, God picked Jackson Cooper? Why not someone like James Wilkins, the nice teacher who had asked her to lunch on occasion?

Why not the very handsome coach from the Tulsa school where she'd taught?

She pulled up to her mailbox and pulled the mail out, shuffling through the letters, junk mail and an electric bill. Another card from her mother. She tossed the mail, all of it, on the seat next to her?

Why another card? Wasn't one unopened card at Christmas enough? Didn't the lack of a response tell her mother what she needed to know, that Madeline had no interest in a relationship with her?

Madeline pulled up her driveway and parked. She sat for a long time, not wanting to move. She wanted to run again. But she wouldn't. She looked at her little house, now adorned with Christmas lights and two new motion lights.

People in Dawson cared. They wanted her in their lives. Jackson Cooper had installed security lights to make her feel safe. She had a church family and neighbors. She picked up her mother's card but she wouldn't open it, not yet.

Instead she forced herself out of the car into the cold December day that gusted and blew. The cold went right through her and she shivered down into her coat.

When she walked into her house she was slammed by more changes. Kid stuff. Jade had left dirty dishes on the counter. Madeline quickly washed them and put them away. A towel had been left on the bedroom floor.

She tossed it in the hamper, wiped the sink and tub and then made the bed in the spare bedroom.

Neat and tidy, everything in its place. She turned to the sound of whimpering. They'd left the puppy on the screened-in back porch. Madeline groaned, knowing this wouldn't be pleasant.

The rug had been chewed to pieces, as had her slippers that she'd left on the floor. The stink of it made her gag and she backed away. The puppy whimpered and plopped down, resting her little head on big paws. Madeline glared at the little renegade.

"No messes in my house, puppy." She pushed the dog aside and reached in the cabinet for paper towels. "My house, my life, is neat and tidy, not messy."

The puppy did a little dance around her feet, barking and nipping at her boots.

"You really don't care, do you?" She leaned to pet the fluff ball. "Neither does he. He doesn't care that I don't want my world turned upside down. No, he brought you, and a child."

He'd pushed his way into her life, her thoughts, her dreams. No one belonged in those places. Dawson had been her safe place. Until last week.

She stomped into the kitchen for a spray bottle of the strongest cleaner she had. The puppy whined at the door.

"Oh, *now* you want to go outside?" She pushed the door open and watched the little dog race outside.

It chased blowing leaves, sniffed grass and then found a stick to chew on. Madeline pulled on rubber gloves, held her breath and started to clean the mess that should have been Jackson Cooper's to clean. Yeah, she should call him and tell him to come down and clean up after his rotten puppy.

If it hadn't meant having him in her home, all male and smelling good, she would have. But she didn't want his faded jeans and cute grin cluttering up the place that way.

Tires squealed and she heard a horrible yelp. The puppy. She tossed the cleaner and paper towels and ran out the front door. A truck sat in the middle of the road and an older man had picked up the puppy.

Jade's puppy. Her puppy. The stupid, sweet, messy puppy.

"I think she's okay." The farmer, a neighbor named Clark, held the ball of fur. "I tried to stop but she was chasing something."

The puppy whimpered and stared with dark eyes. Her little body trembled. "I should take her to a vet."

"I think you probably should. I'm real sorry. She came out of nowhere."

Madeline closed her eyes to the surge of tears. "I let her out. I didn't think about her running across the road."

She didn't know a vet. She didn't know anything about dogs. Or cats. Or cows.

"Let me put her in your car." The farmer, in bib overalls and a straw cowboy hat, trudged through the ditch and up the hill. "Do you know where to take her?"

"I'll figure it out."

"Doc Marler is good. If you can catch him."

She nodded and her mind spun in crazy circles trying to think about dogs and vets and what to tell Jade. A new batch of tears streamed down her cheeks. She'd have to tell Jade.

"I think she'll be okay. And if you send me the vet bill, I'd be happy to pay it."

Madeline rubbed the useless, silly tears from her

eyes. "No, I'm the one who let her out and didn't watch her."

"Well, you let me know how she is. She's a cute little pup."

"She is, isn't she?" Madeline sighed and shook her head. "I didn't know I wanted a dog."

The farmer left the dog in her car and headed back down the driveway. Her cell phone rang. She pulled it from her pocket and groaned when she saw the caller ID. She didn't need this, not right now. And then, she did. Because he would know what to do.

She answered her phone with a quick hello and then said, "The puppy got hit by a car. I don't know what to do."

Her body trembled the way the puppy trembled. The poor little thing hunkered in her front seat, holding her front leg out.

"I'll be right there." Jackson's voice over the cell phone undid a little of the fear. He wouldn't leave her alone to handle this. Of course he wouldn't. He helped everyone. He rebuilt tornado-damaged homes and searched for missing children.

When he pulled up a few minutes later, she breathed a little easier. Jackson jumped out of his truck and headed her way. His smile shot clean through her, tender and unexpected. And she started to cry.

"Hey now, what's this all about?" His voice had a huskiness that undid every last shred of calm. "The puppy is going to be fine. Look at her, she's getting all worried about you."

Madeline nodded but she couldn't stop the tears. Everything inside her broke loose and she couldn't shove it all back inside. The puppy whimpered and belly-crawled to the edge of her car seat.

"Shh, you're okay." Jackson pulled her to him and held her in strong arms. "Shh."

She sobbed against his shoulder and knew that the strange calm seeping into her body, into her heart, was from him. Safe. And suddenly, not so safe.

"I thought she was dead." Make it about the dog, much easier to make it about something other than the Grand Canyon splitting open inside her heart.

"A puppy against a truck. She beat the odds today." He still held her. His lips brushed her hair and he didn't let go.

"Jade will be so upset."

"She's fine. I called and she's going to stay the night with Heather. Doc is waiting for us."

"Thank you." Madeline moved from his arms, brushing her hand across her face. "I'm a mess. And I need to run inside and get my purse."

"You aren't a mess." He brushed hair from her face. "Get what you need and I'll put her in my truck."

She nodded and rushed back into the house for her purse. She turned off lights on her way out and locked the front door. When she got to the truck Jackson had the door open for her.

The puppy crawled close, head resting on Madeline's leg. She looked quickly at the man sitting next to her. A friend. He had said it himself. They were friends.

The local veterinarian had been in town most of Jackson's life. He had even delivered a baby once, years ago. It had been a stormy night and the woman, a dairy farmer's wife, had gone into labor while Doc had been there taking care of a sick cow. When things had moved a little too quickly, Doc delivered Jasmine Porter.

Jackson parked and got out. Madeline, still pale and

shaken, held Angel in her lap. He'd heard her murmur a few prayers, even promise the dog that she did like her and was glad she had her. He smiled as he helped the two of them out of the truck.

"You know, you didn't do this to the dog."

"I was really angry that she chewed up my rug and made a mess in the utility room."

"So every time a dog's owner gets mad, God sends a truck to teach them a lesson?" He kind of chuckled, and she shot him a look that took the humor right out of the moment.

"It isn't funny."

"It kind of is, if you think about it. I don't think life works that way. I don't think God works that way. He doesn't get us back every time we have a thought He doesn't approve of."

"I know." She smiled a little. "I know it's a crazy thought. I'm a woman, we get at least three crazy thoughts a week."

"I'll try to remember that." He opened the door and she went through, still holding the puppy she hadn't really wanted. He smiled as he followed her inside. He couldn't stop smiling.

Something must have happened to him when he got tossed off that horse. Maybe he'd hit his head and they hadn't realized.

A door to the left of the desk opened. Doc walked out, slipping into a pale green jacket as he did. He nodded at Madeline and the dog before turning to Jackson.

"How old?"

"Eight weeks, Doc. Looks like her front leg."

Doc's bushy gray brows shot up. "You're a vet now?"

Jackson laughed. "Doc, you're more than a vet."

"Yeah, I'm the guy that…"

Ran Jackson off when he took Doc's daughter out a few times. But since Doc had the only veterinary clinic in Dawson, they'd worked past the resentment.

Doc took the puppy from Madeline.

"I'll take it back for X-rays. You two stay here."

Madeline stood in the center of the room, looking a lot like a woman letting go of a kid for the first time. Jackson looped his arm through hers. "I'll buy you a cupcake if you'll stop looking so guilty."

He led her to the vending machines at the end of the room.

"What kind?" He pulled a few ones out of his wallet.

"I love cinnamon rolls."

He fed the dollar into the machine and pushed the button. The package of cinnamon rolls dropped down and she reached in and grabbed them. "Thank you."

"Something to drink?"

Madeline shrugged. "Water. I'm so sorry that I dragged you over here. I know you're tired and still trying to heal up. And you have other things to do. You have a life."

Pink flooded her cheeks and he grinned at the rush of random words that spilled from her lips.

"I do have a life." He fed a dollar into the machine and pushed the button for a bottle of water.

"I mean, you know…"

He laughed. "You mean…women?"

"You know what I mean. Don't make me say it."

"Dating women is something I do enjoy. I'm a single man. That makes it okay."

"Right, I know that." She took her cinnamon rolls and the bottle of water back to one of the hard plastic chairs that lined the wall near the door. "I'm apologizing because I know this is keeping you from your life. I can't even, I don't know…"

He sat down next to her. "You can't, you don't what?"

"I could have called Jenna or Beth. I have friends. I do have a life." She glanced at her watch. "I have play practice in two hours."

"I know you have a life."

"I just panicked and when you called, I blurted it out."

"And I offered." He couldn't tell her the truth, that he liked being the person who came to her rescue. "Don't worry, she'll be fine and as soon as she's taken care of, we'll head over to Back Street."

"We?"

"I have some work to do over there."

"Oh, okay." She reached for her purse and pulled out a stack of mail. Her face paled a little and she looked away, shoving the letters back into the side pocket of her bag.

"Bad news?"

She shook her head and she her shoulders slumped. "My mother sent me another card."

"What does it say?"

"I didn't open it. I don't open them."

"Why?"

She looked up at him, staring as if she thought he'd dropped off another planet. Okay, maybe he should get this, but he didn't. Women weren't the most understandable creatures in the world. Beautiful, nice to hold, but definitely not easy to understand.

"Why would I open it?" She held it in her hands and he wanted to take it from her, open it himself.

"Because you need to."

"That sounds easy." She smiled up at him. "So, just open this card and, 'tah-dah,' everything is better?"

"No, but I think it would be a beginning. Look, Maddie, I know that my family looks pretty great from the outside, but we've had our problems and we've learned that it's best to take care of situations from the get-go. Don't let it drag on. Don't let it take root."

"It's already rooted, Jackson. This is more like having to weed a garden that's been let go."

"I understand."

She put her hand on the edge of the card and tore just a little. "This isn't easy."

"No, I bet it isn't. But remember, the only thing in there are words, and if you don't like them, toss them in the trash, burn them, never open another card from her."

"Right." She slid her finger under the flap and pulled out a Christmas card.

Emotions flickered across her face as she read. Jackson watched, waiting, not pushing. She bit down on her bottom lip and then her eyes closed briefly. Finally she shrugged and handed him the card.

"She was pregnant, sixteen and living on the streets. She thought Rainbow Valley sounded peaceful, like a place to raise a baby."

"Are you glad you read the card?"

"It changes things." She took the card back, looked it over again and then slid it into the envelope. "But it doesn't change what happened. It doesn't answer the other questions. Now I have more questions. Why didn't she leave?"

"I guess those are questions only she can answer. But maybe not questions to answer in a card."

"Sara wasn't really my sister."

Jackson moved his arm, encircling her slim shoulders and pulling her close. Two weeks ago she'd been a neighbor, not even a friend.

"Maddie, did you ever think that the two of us would be sitting here together sharing huge events in each other's lives?"

"Never."

He laughed at her strong response. "You make it sound like the worst thing that could have happened to you."

She looked up and took him by surprise. Her hand touched his cheek, rested there and then moved to his shoulder. "It hasn't been the worst thing at all."

The door opened and Doc walked out, carrying the injured puppy. His weathered gaze shot from Madeline to Jackson and he shook his head. "Some things never change. Here's the dog. And here's the bill."

"Is she going to be okay?" Madeline touched the dog's back.

Doc handed Jackson the slip of paper. "A broken leg, but she'll heal quickly enough. You paying?"

"I can…" Madeline reached for the bill.

Jackson shook his head. "No, I'll pay for this."

Madeline took the puppy and held her close. The same puppy she hadn't been too fond of yesterday. Jackson wrote out a check for the vet bill and walked her out the door.

"What's the deal between you and Doc?" she asked as Jackson opened the truck door for her.

"He caught me parking with his daughter about sixteen years ago and he has a long memory." Jackson waited for her to get in the truck and then he leaned in close. "And back then he had a pretty good aim with his shotgun."

Jackson moved his arm, c

es off my truck. I had a hard
to my dad."

walked around to the driver's
over time and with numerous
vas still the truth. And maybe
Madeline why he was the last
me connected with.

e too late to be thinking about

you.

She looked up and took h
touched his cheek, rested the
shoulder. "It hasn't been the s

The door opened and Doc
turned again. His weathered
to Jackson and he shook his h
change. Here's the dog. And I

"Is she going to be okay?"

dog's back.

Doc handed Jackson the sh
but she'd heal quietly enough

"I can—" Madeline reache

Jackson shook his head. "I

Madeline took the puppy
same puppy, she hadn't seen to
you wrote out a check for the
out the door.

anyhow's the deal between
as Jackson opened the truck d

The couple negotiating wi
teen years ago and he was a
waited for her to get in the tru
closer. And back then he had
his shotgun.

Chapter Eleven

Dawson Community Church cancelled Wednesday-night services. With just three weeks until Christmas and less than two weeks before the living nativity was scheduled to begin, it was decided they needed more practice, so everyone involved would meet at Dawson Community Center. Madeline had planned on picking Jade up after school but Jackson told her he'd bring her with him.

Madeline pulled into the community center parking lot shortly before six. People were already there. Lights had been plugged in outside, huge shop lights with bright halogen bulbs. She walked up to the building, searching the crowds for that familiar face.

Searching for Jackson. She shook her head and told herself to stop. Before long Jade would be going back to her mother. Jackson would go back to his life and she'd go back to living in her empty house, uncluttered, unencumbered, empty. And she would be happy for that day to come.

Really she would.

"Madeline."

She turned quickly, spotted Jade and smiled. "You have ketchup on your chin."

Jade scrubbed at her face with her hand. "Better?"

"Yeah, sure." Madeline rubbed away the last smudge of ketchup. "What did you have for dinner?"

"Jackson made corn dogs."

"Nice." She turned, saw Jackson walk through the door and averted her gaze, returning her attention to the girl in front of her. "Did you have a good day?"

"Yeah, but he's a grouch."

Madeline nodded and decided to let it go. "Come downstairs with me. I have to get dressed and you can hang with me. If you want?"

"Yeah, I want. How's the puppy?"

"Same as this morning, pitiful. I think she isn't as bad as she wants us to think."

Jade laughed at that. "I think she loves the attention." And then the girl's smile faded. "I'm going to miss her."

Because this weekend they were going to Oklahoma City to try and find her mother. "I know, but you'll get to see her again."

"When?" Jade walked next to her, small and slim, a kid who worked hard at being strong.

"Soon. I promise."

"Right."

Madeline turned to the girl. "Jade, I keep my promises."

"Yeah, probably."

"Hey, where are you two going?" Jackson appeared next to Madeline.

"Downstairs to get dressed. Don't you have something to build?" Madeline had realized something lately. She didn't know how to have an easygoing conversation with a man. She tried but it came out more like an order, less like banter.

"I do have work to do. I'll catch up with you later."

Madeline nodded and then he left. She ignored Jade's knowing glances and headed downstairs. Next to her Jade giggled.

"What's so funny?"

"The two of you, acting like you don't like each other or like you haven't been spending a lot of time together."

"We haven't been spending time…" Okay, they had, but not because they wanted to. He had made her a cup of tea Monday after they got home from the vet. He'd listened as she told him little details about her childhood. He'd given advice about finding Sara.

"Yeah, you like him," Jade teased.

"No, I don't. I mean, I do, but not…" She groaned at the direction the conversation had taken. "Jade, I'm not discussing this with you."

"Fine, that's okay. But can you do me a favor?"

They were in the kitchen of the community center, surrounded by people, and Madeline didn't know if she wanted to continue the conversation around so many pairs of ears. But Jade's hazel eyes locked with hers, begging.

"What is it?"

"Tell him to keep me. I'm his daughter and I can't go back."

"Jade, I can't make this decision for him."

"Then you keep me. Call family services and tell them that my mom isn't fit. You're a teacher, they'll believe you."

"I can't do that."

"Of course not. If I hadn't messed up and gotten the

address wrong, you'd still be doing your own thing and you wouldn't be bothered with us."

Madeline hugged the girl. "Yes, I would still have my uncomplicated, uncluttered life. I would be sitting alone in the evening in a quiet house with no one to talk to."

Although a little silence would be nice. With Jade in her home, in her life, silence seemed to be a thing of the past. When Jade left, would Jackson also be a thing of the past?

"I need to get in costume." She brushed off the thoughts that didn't make sense.

"What do I do?" Jade followed her into the dressing room.

"You can come with me and watch."

Jade sat down on a stool and watched as Madeline got ready.

"A woman called my da…" Jade looked down and shrugged. "Called Jackson today."

"Jade, that's personal." Madeline tied the fabric belt around the waist of the costume.

"Yeah, I guess. I heard him tell her he couldn't see her right now. And I think she must have asked when he could see her and he said he didn't think he'd be seeing her anytime soon."

Madeline pretended she wasn't listening because hadn't she just said that this information was personal? She didn't need to know what Jackson told women that called his home. Honestly, she didn't care.

Much.

Jackson slid the paper with the DNA results back into his pocket along with the other medical information. He had work to do. There were people everywhere.

He sighed and walked through the crowd to the back of the manger. He'd been helping with the star, getting it in place so that it would shine over Bethlehem and the baby Jesus.

Beautiful Star of Bethlehem. He could almost hear his great grandmother singing the song. The memory brought a smile and he hadn't had much to smile about today. He had a lot to think about.

When he turned from the tower holding the star he saw Madeline and Jade walking together, heads bent toward one another, whispering and smiling. He smiled, seeing the two of them together. Yeah, he had a lot to think about.

Later he'd talk to Madeline. He stopped working for a minute to think about that decision. He'd been thinking about her all day, thinking about talking to her, about telling her his news, how his day had gone.

And then he'd anticipated her reaction to the medical tests and the secret he didn't want to share. He watched her walk into place, surrounded by sheep. Jade watched from a short distance away.

Someone walked up behind him. He turned, nodded and tipped his hat to Wyatt Johnson. Wyatt grinned big and turned his attention from Jackson to Madeline, back to Jackson

"Watch out, that one will get under your skin." Wyatt Johnson smirked a little. Payback for what Jackson had told him last year.

"I don't think so, Wyatt."

Wyatt laughed, loud. People turned to stare and Wyatt thumped him on the back, jolting him and making him flinch a little.

"Watch the ribs, if you don't mind." Jackson rolled his shoulders to unkink the muscles.

"That's right, you got tossed last week. You aren't the first guy around here with some broken ribs."

"I'm not as young as I used to be." He grimaced, knowing he sounded way too much like a country song.

"Right, you're not. So what's wrong with taking time to get to know one of the nicest single females in this town?" Wyatt watched his own wife head their way. Something stabbed at Jackson's heart. Jealousy? Nah, couldn't be.

"Nothing wrong with it, Wyatt. But I think she's a little out of my league."

"She probably is." Wyatt raised his hand to thump Jackson on the back a second time and Jackson moved to the side.

"Could you not?"

"Oh, sorry, didn't know you were so weak."

"Right, weak."

"You're not your normal humorous self." Wyatt turned to watch the beginning of the living nativity as it got underway. His voice lowered. "Seriously, is there anything I can do to help?"

"No, not right now." Jackson shoved his hands in his pocket, feeling the paper that he'd gotten that day. "I'm good."

"Well, it was good to see you in church on Sunday. You plan on coming back this Sunday?"

"No." He had to explain, not leave Wyatt hanging. Although that would have been fun. He watched the progression of Mary on the donkey, Joseph at her side.

He finally turned and smiled at Wyatt who had the good sense not to push, but he looked pretty tense with all of those unasked questions rolling around inside him.

"Wyatt, I'll be back. I'm taking Jade to Oklahoma

City this weekend." He watched Mary and Joseph exit the inn, looking young and perplexed. "But I'm coming back. I guess I got tired of going and having to face questions, a few accusing looks, my own guilt."

"So what's changed?"

Jackson didn't mean to but he looked in the direction of Jade. And Madeline. He tried to brush it off, to pretend it had nothing to do with either of them. It really did have more to do with him.

"I guess a guy has to face his life. Time to make some changes."

"She's a cute kid."

Jackson nodded but didn't say more. Yeah, Jade was cute. She looked like him. She had his eyes. Sometimes it looked as if she had his smile.

"She's great," Jackson agreed. She had somehow survived a childhood that hadn't been much of a childhood and a mother who hadn't been a mother.

He refocused on Madeline as a shepherdess. As he watched the angels appeared. Madeline went down on her knees, covering her head with her arm. Jackson walked away from Wyatt. He walked closer to the scene of the shepherds leaving the field and walking toward the manger. He stood close as Mary revealed her newborn son and angels began to sing. The shepherds bowed at her feet.

Jackson stood there waiting for normal to return. But it wouldn't and he knew that. He'd changed. Maybe this was the new normal? Maybe this was his new life? Something had to be wrong with him. He'd turned down a date today with a woman he'd gone out with off and on for the last two years. She was a lawyer's daughter and owned a clothing boutique in Tulsa. She was uncomplicated.

He'd turned her down because of the shepherdess kneeling not ten feet from him. The same shepherdess who looked up at that moment and caught him staring. Yeah, he was definitely losing control of his life.

Jade saw him standing there, watching. She smiled big and bounced away from the group she'd been crowded in with. A kid who thought she was his. He thought about her future and it left a pretty big space in his heart because she deserved a home, a life with people who cared about her.

Tomorrow he would try again to contact her mother. And if he couldn't, then what? He had a load of bulls to take to Oklahoma City. He could try to find her. But he couldn't keep Jade indefinitely. He couldn't expect Madeline to raise her. He'd considered talking to his parents.

But this one was in his court.

The program ended. Jade stood at his side, a skinny kid in a big, puffy coat. Her cheeks were pink from the cold and her nose was red. She smiled up at him.

"This is great." Her tone was all happiness and sunshine.

"Yeah, it is." He pulled her close to his side for an instant and thought about moments in the future and how it would change everything for her.

"Is it time to go now?"

He nodded and watched as Madeline spoke to a few people and then slipped away from the crowd. He watched her. He couldn't stop watching her. He smiled as she walked toward him, toward Jade.

"That was great." He thought about the three of them, arm in arm, leaving together.

"Thank you. It feels as if it is all coming together."

"Yeah, it does." He felt Jade move away from him,

but he couldn't stop staring at the woman in a shepherd's costume. He couldn't stop thinking about holding her close, making her feel safe.

"I'm going inside." Jade punched his arm. "They're serving hot chocolate and cookies."

"Go for it. We'll leave soon," he called out after her. She raised a hand to let him know she'd heard. It made him feel like a dad. Strange, really strange that it could happen so easily, this change in his life.

"Are you okay?" Madeline stood in front of him still. She had zeroed in on his mood. She knew how to do that and it unnerved him a little.

"I'm good." He didn't reach into his pocket for the piece of paper. "I'm going to try again to contact her mother. If I can't, I have to drive down there and look for her."

Madeline's gaze drifted to the church, to the door Jade had just skipped through. "I know. It's a shame though. I mean, I know I can't keep her, but I wish she could stay."

He reached for Madeline's hand. "Let's walk."

"Oh, okay." She hesitated, glancing toward the church. Small crowds gathered in front of the building, talking. A few people looked their way.

Yeah, rumors, gossip. He knew the drill.

"We can talk later," he said, because he didn't want to give people a reason to talk.

"Is this about Jade?"

He nodded once and released her hand. When he did she touched his arm. It would have been easy to hold on to her, to make this about him, not about Jade. But it was about Jade. In the short span of a week his life had become all about a kid.

And a woman.

was he should escape.

ugh his. He knew that
asy gestures weren't
ok real courage. He
eaned to drop a kiss

midst of gossip and

afraid?"

a breathless way and
ression matched. She
ring in her eyes.
ld Jackson to get hold
nises, Maddie."
e turned, still holding
he church. She didn't

Chapter Twelve

The phone rang and rang as Madeline unlocked her front door. She tried to hurry but her fingers were numb from cold. Jade stood next to her, hopping up and down a little. The wind whipped against them, a cold, north wind.

Finally she pushed the door opened and they rushed into the warmth of the living room, greeted by wood smoke and Angel barking from the laundry room. Jade ran past her, heading for the dog, of course. She could hear the girl calling to the animal as she hurried through the house.

"Don't throw clothes everywhere," Madeline warned and then in a quieter voice because it didn't matter added, "I have a hall tree."

She hung her coat and kicked out of her boots before picking up the phone and checking the caller ID. The number didn't look familiar. It didn't have a local area code. She pushed the number for voicemail and listened. Her heart raced as the message played and then she slammed the phone down.

Not at Christmas. She didn't want to do this at Christmas. Forgiveness needed to happen, she got that.

She even thought she had forgiven. But she didn't want her mother forcing her way into this life, a safe life with safe people.

Her world had already been upended by a young girl and a confirmed bachelor who wanted safe help. She was safe. Her life was safe. She plopped down in the big easy chair she'd bought when she first moved in.

The perfect chair for quiet evenings alone, reading a book, drinking tea. Safe.

Loud laughter reminded her she didn't have a quiet evening ahead of her. Then footsteps. Jade ran into the room carrying the puppy that licked and licked her face.

"She's glad to see you." Madeline smiled in spite of herself. Being alone was overrated. Jade made noise and clutter worth it.

This weekend the girl would be gone. Madeline's heart broke a little for her, because she knew how it hurt to be jerked around at that age. Maybe she'd keep Jade. Maybe she'd file for custody if Jackson didn't plan on doing something.

Why wouldn't he? He was her dad. He had to do something.

"Can I go to work with you tomorrow?" Jade plopped down on the sofa with the dog.

"I can't take you to work with me." She would have loved to. Jade needed to be in school. "Jackson is going to spend the day with you. He has a lot of work to do, he said, and you can help."

"Oh, that's cool." Jade leaned in for the puppy to lick her face again. "I love this dog. I've never had one."

Madeline smiled as she watched dog and child. "Me, neither. I think you love her more than I do."

"Do you love my da…" Madeline's heart broke a

little more for Jade, even if this did sound like a tricky question coming at her. "Jackson?"

"We should go to bed." Cop-out.

Jade hugged the puppy and giggled. "She needs to go outside. And you do love him."

"I don't. Jade, love is more complicated and takes more than two people being thrown together. It is more than just simple emotions. It's about two people being connected, really caring about each other. It's about wanting to share lives and everything, good or bad, that goes with life. It takes time to find and build a love like that."

"I think you could love each other, get married and we'd be a family." Jade's tone was wistful and sad. "Don't you think?"

Madeline sighed because she didn't know what to say. She let her heart trip over the idea of being in love with Jackson Cooper. Complicated. He made her life way too complicated, and she avoided complicated as often as possible.

"I think it really is bedtime. You're so tired you're delirious." Madeline pushed herself out of her favorite chair and reached for Jade's hand. "It's cold but the puppy has to go outside."

Jade giggled. "Too late. You should see your laundry room."

"I'm seriously going to make Jackson Cooper come over here and clean up the mess. By the time this is over he's going to owe me a new floor."

"Yep, you love him."

She swatted Jade, a playful swat. "Give me the dog and you go brush your teeth."

All of the right mom words were coming out. It took her by surprise that she knew those things to say, because she'd never had a mother who said them. And now her mother wanted to be in her life.

No. Madeline couldn't go there. She could forgive, but letting the woman in her life, that she couldn't do. Jade headed into the hall but she stopped and glanced back.

"Are you okay?" The girl bit down on her bottom lip and her eyes, so much like Jackson's, studied Madeline's face with intensity that unnerved.

"I'm good, just tired."

"Okay, I'll brush my teeth." Jade smiled a sweet smile. "I think he could love you back."

"Jade, go." Madeline cringed on the inside. That definitely sounded like a mom voice.

The phone rang again. Madeline held the puppy in her arms and stared at the caller ID. The same number. She closed her eyes and waited for it to stop ringing. Slowly her hand descended, picking it up. Because she wouldn't run anymore. She couldn't. She had to face the past to move on with her life.

"Hello?"

"Madeline? It's me. It's your mother."

Madeline's world went dark for a moment. It spun. It faded and then righted itself. The puppy licked her face. She set her down on the floor and held the phone against her ear.

"Madeline?"

"I'm here." *Breathe. Breathe.* She leaned against the wall, trying to block images of her mother's face, smiling, telling her it would be okay. But it wasn't okay. Her mother led her to the man who abused her. Tore her life apart. Her mother waited for her. Held her. Told her she was sorry.

Sorry?

"I know you don't want to talk to me."

"Really, so why are you calling?" Madeline sank to the floor. The puppy crawled into her lap. Jackson had been right about having a dog.

"I'm calling because I have to. I need to." Her mother sobbed from hundreds of miles away. "I'm in Tulsa."

"No." Not hundreds of miles. Tulsa. A little more than an hour's drive. "No."

She waited but the world kept spinning. Faster and faster.

"I want to see you."

"No." She couldn't get another word out. She couldn't form another response. She couldn't even tell the woman on the other end to go away.

Because a part of her still wanted a mother? Because she knew she needed to forgive?

But not this woman. Not now.

"Madeline, I was young. I made mistakes."

"Mistakes?" Madeline shuddered as she released a breath. "Mistakes are something a person makes in their checkbook. Mistakes are when you say the wrong thing or buy the wrong car. Those are mistakes. You didn't make a mistake. You allowed your only daughter to be abused."

"I know." A long silence, sobbing on the other end that Madeline couldn't be sorry for. But she was. "I hurt you. I wanted you to know that I was afraid, too."

"Oh, okay, well, thank you for sharing that. I'm sorry you were afraid."

"This isn't going well."

Madeline closed her eyes and tears slid down her cheeks.

"No, it isn't. I can't talk to you right now."

"Maybe soon? I have a job and an apartment in Tulsa. I wanted to be close to you so I moved here."

"I have to go." Madeline hung up.

A few minutes later Jade kneeled in front of her. She didn't take the dog. Instead she curled close and hugged Madeline. "Are you okay?"

Madeline nodded. She tried to smile and reassure Jade, but she couldn't. Her heart ached. Her throat tightened with the tears, the emotion. She wanted to crawl inside herself, the way she'd done as a teenager. She wanted to hide from the pain and close herself off from feeling.

But she couldn't go back. God had done too much in her life. She couldn't go back to being the person who hid from life.

Jade hugged her hard and let go. "I'll be back."

Madeline nodded. She knew Jade walked away. The puppy, limping and hopping, followed. Madeline hugged her knees close to her chest and took a deep breath. She had to get it together.

She needed to take care of Jade, not let the girl take care of her. She leaned her head on her knees and prayed for strength to get through whatever her mother would throw at her in the coming weeks. She prayed for strength to truly forgive.

And then the front door opened. Madeline looked up. Jade stood nearby. She pointed at Madeline and Jackson nodded. In the blink of an eye Jade disappeared and Jackson was at her side. He leaned and lifted her into his arms.

"Why are you here?" Madeline leaned into his shoulder, finding it hard to believe that he had showed up when he did. Jade had called him, of course she had.

And he was here. Her heart wanted to open up like a flower in early spring reaching for the sun.

He carried her to the couch and sat down with her held against him, his arms strong and holding her close to his side. She closed her eyes. This is what safe feels like, she told herself. To be held.

She thought of all the times God had held her. Through the toughest times of her life. Held and kept her anchored in faith.

"Jade called. She was worried."

"I'm fine." And then she cried. She flooded his shirt with her tears and he stroked her hair and told her everything would be okay.

She believed him.

"What happened?" He reached for the tissue box on her table and handed it to her, but he didn't stop holding her, making her feel safe.

"Do I have to talk about this?"

"Not if you don't want to." He wrapped her in protective arms and held her tight. She leaned into his strength and she couldn't force herself to move.

"My mother has not only found me, she called and she's living in Tulsa. She'll be there when I decide I want her in my life."

Jackson sighed. She felt the rise and fall of his chest. His hand slid down her back. "I know this isn't easy, but I know that you're strong. And you know I'll be here."

"I know." Did she? Why would he be here for her? She couldn't ask those questions. For the moment she had someone in her life who promised to be there for her.

Jade had asked her if she loved him. No, of course not. She was a grown woman. She knew better than to think she'd fallen in love with him. They'd been thrown together for a short time because of a teenager and a dog. They'd somehow forged a friendship.

"Maddie, I mean it." His voice, soft and husky, warm near her ear. She wasn't in love with Jackson. Attracted to him, definitely. But love?

She looked up, intending to tell him something brave and witty, if only she could think of something. When her lips parted he leaned and met her with a kiss that made her forget doubts, fears, pain. He brushed her lips with his, feather-soft, once, twice. She clung to him, exploring this moment, no fear, no desire to run, only a need to stay in his arms. His lips touched hers again, lingering this time.

The dog barked; Jackson pulled away. His eyes widened a little and he smiled. "Maddie, Maddie, you do push a man to forget his convictions."

"Right, Jackson, that's me, the temptress."

They both laughed and he pulled her close. "More than you know."

The dog hopped into the room. A moment later Jade followed, a knowing little grin on her face. "I'm going to bed."

Jackson stood and pulled the girl into an easy hug. He kissed the top of her head and ruffled her hair. "Thanks for calling me."

"Anytime." Jade's gaze dropped to Madeline. "I took the dog out."

The evidence was in her face. The pink cheeks. The red nose. Her eyes glistened a little.

"Jade, are you okay?"

Jade nodded. "I'm good."

Madeline patted the couch next to her and Jade plopped down. Madeline hugged her tight. "It really is going to be okay."

"I know it is. Right?" Jade looked up at Jackson.

Madeline followed the look and what she saw frightened her. Jackson put on a good front. He smiled and Jade probably believed him, that everything would be okay. The look in his eyes, a look he sent Madeline, told her otherwise.

Jade seemed convinced. "Good night."

The girl hurried down the hall, the dog trying to follow.

"What's going on?" Madeline asked as Jackson paced her floor.

Jackson pulled a piece of paper from his pocket and tossed it her way. He put a finger to his lips and she got it. Everything wasn't okay. He sat down next to her again.

What she read slammed her heart. She knew he must have felt this way or worse when he read the results. The DNA test showed that Jade Baker could not be Jackson Cooper's biological daughter.

She didn't know what to say.

Madeline handed him back the paper and she couldn't look at him, couldn't see the sadness in his eyes. Or would it be relief?

When she did look at him, she saw concern and worry, not relief. It made her heart soar a little.

"Now what?"

"I'm not sure what to do." He rubbed the back of his neck and then leaned back on the sofa, closing his eyes.

Madeline didn't know what to say. She reached for his hand and waited, because he needed time and she knew he needed a friend. A friend. He had those. He had family. And he was sitting next to her, on her couch, lost.

"Jackson, we have to find her mother." She held his hand tight, wishing she could do more.

His thumb brushed her fingers. "Yeah, I know. Thank you for being a part of this. 'We' sounds much better than me, alone."

She wondered about that. He seemed good at being alone.

"Of course I'll do what I can. I love her, too."

"I know." He let out a long sigh. "I have to tell her she isn't mine. And I have to take her back to Oklahoma City to her mother."

"I'll go with you." The words rushed out. Jackson's hand tightened on hers. He lifted it and held her palm to his lips.

He moved to the edge of the couch, leaning for a moment over clasped hands. Madeline's hand rested on his back and he turned, smiling.

"And I have to go now. Because you're amazing and I…should really go."

She followed him to the door, trying to figure out the sudden change.

"Maddie…" He leaned and kissed her goodbye, soft and slow, ending with a sigh as he walked away.

Madeline wanted to run after him. She wanted to call him a coward for running. She was the one who ran but she hadn't. This time she hadn't run. She hadn't hidden inside herself.

She watched him drive away, headlights in the dark night. Somewhere a coyote howled. She could hear trucks on the distant highway. Lost, she stood there in the cold of the open door because Jade might have a point. A teenager understood Madeline's feelings better than she understood them herself.

* * *

Jackson fired up the tractor the next morning and hooked a round bale to take out to the cattle in the back pasture. Madeline hadn't gotten there yet with Jade but Travis had shown up and he'd be in the barn when they arrived.

He drove along the fenceline, stopping to open a gate when he got to the field where they were grazing the beef cattle. He hopped back in the tractor and eased it through, then got out to close the gate again. He latched it tight because he had no intention of chasing down a hundred plus head of cattle today. Sleet had started to fall an hour earlier. Nothing major but enough to make the cold pretty miserable.

As he climbed back in the tractor he heard a pitiful sound. He stood on the step and looked around but didn't see anything out of the ordinary. The cattle were a good hundred yards out. They were grouped together, fighting the wind and sleet. As he headed their way they started to move. He'd brought a bale out yesterday but he planned on moving several bales today. He also needed to corral the young bulls he would be selling this weekend to a breeder just outside of Oklahoma City.

The City, as it was more popularly referred to. When someone was going to the City, everyone knew what they meant—Oklahoma City.

A dark form in the grass caught his attention. He lowered the bale of hay and backed off from it. The cattle were already moving in, even though they still had hay. He'd need to check the automatic waterer, to make sure it wasn't frozen.

He hated the cold. Even in the enclosed tractor, complete with heat, he felt it down to his bones. The wind whistled. Maybe the sound of the wind made it seem even colder. Whatever, he was ready for spring already and winter hadn't really hit yet.

The dark shape moved and he saw that it was a calf. The form next to it didn't move. He headed the tractor in that direction. Not a good morning for a downed cow. As he got closer the cow still didn't move. She didn't even raise her head.

Even worse. He jumped down from the idling tractor and eased toward the bawling calf. Cold air gusted, blowing against him. The calf appeared to be a few hours old, and half frozen. The sleet coated its dark fur, still wet, but icy.

"Not a good way to start your life, little guy." He scooped up the bawling calf, took a last look at the momma cow to make sure his assumption was correct.

She was gone. He walked away, holding the calf. Part of farm life. Yeah, he knew that. He'd learned the lesson early in life. Sometimes animals died. People died. He guessed for some people it got easier.

He reached to open the tractor door and pushed the calf inside the cab, following it. "Now what in the world are we going to do with you?"

A few minutes later the tractor rolled toward the barn and he knew what he'd do with this calf. Madeline's car parked in front of the barn gave him the answer he needed. He drove past the barn to the equipment barn. Tractors, an old farm truck and a couple of stock trailers were parked under the roof of the three-sided, open-front building.

Jade ran toward him as he got out of the tractor and headed for the barn. She didn't seem to notice the cold and he remembered how his grandfather had always said that cold got colder as a man got older. He grinned, remembering.

"A calf!" Jade's eyes lit up. "Where's its mom?"

"Gone." He didn't want to say more. He didn't want to see her eyes full of tears. But he knew it had to happen. Just like eventually he'd have to tell her that she wasn't his.

"What happened?" Madeline had walked up behind Jade. She looked so good this morning, he wanted to grab her up in his arms and thank her for being in his life.

He didn't know who would be more shocked if he did that. Probably better if he let it go. The tender vulnerability in her eyes last night warned him to go easy, move slowly.

Jade was petting the sticky, wet calf.

"I found him with his mother. It happens." He hated that it did. "We need to get him a bottle and get him warmed up."

"He won't die, will he?" Jade's eyes widened as she looked from him to the calf.

"Of course he won't." Jackson led them all into the barn. Travis had left. "Where'd Trav go?"

"He had to get home and start packing for Tulsa." Madeline's voice trailed off when she said the name of the nearest city. "School got cancelled due to the weather."

"Yeah, I can imagine that. Let's get this little guy settled and a few chores done and I'll take you girls to the Mad Cow."

For lunch. And he didn't care what people said or how they talked.

"What can we do?" Madeline followed him into the feed room.

"I'll hold him if you can grab that bottle and mix the calf starter. In that rubber tub, a scoop of the starter and then fill the bottle with water from the sink in the bathroom through that door." He pointed to the door across from them. "Jade, grab a towel out of that cabinet and let's get him dried off."

"Got it." Madeline already had the lid off the tub. Jade pulled a towel from the cabinet and rubbed it over the calf.

"A little harder than that, kiddo. We need to get him dry and warmed up."

"Poor calf," she crooned as she rubbed the calf he'd set on the floor of the feed room. "Everyone should have a mom."

And that sent an arrow to his heart. Every kid should have a family, too. His mom had tried to give a home to as many as possible. He'd learned at an early age that family didn't necessarily have to be about blood connections and DNA.

"Here it is." Madeline returned, a city girl in jeans and a heavy coat, lace-up suede boots to keep her feet warm. She knew how to blend.

She handed him the bottle, her hands covered in crocheted gloves that were probably pretty worthless in the cold, especially if they got wet.

"You need better gloves." He shoved the bottle into the fighting calf's mouth. The calf turned his head one way and then the other. "Hold his head."

"Okay. Why doesn't he want it?"

"It isn't his momma. Give him a minute to realize it's food and he'll take to it."

Madeline held the calf's head and Jackson opened his mouth. The calf let out a little moo and then clamped down on the giant-size baby bottle.

"There he goes."

Jade moved close. "Aww, just like a baby."

Jackson laughed. "Yeah, a baby who will someday weigh close to a ton, have horns and be able to run you into the ground. Don't let him fool you. He isn't a pet."

"But he's cute," Madeline insisted. He'd put the calf on the wood floor and it wagged its tail and pushed against the bottle he had handed over to Jade. Slobber flew, dripped down the calf's chin. Jade laughed and held tight to the bottle.

"He's strong."

"He is strong," Jackson agreed. "And cute. But still, he's going to grow up to be…"

"A big, mean bull." Madeline repeated his warning with a little laugh.

He shot her a smile and watched her cheeks turn pink. Yeah, he hadn't lost it completely.

"Right."

Madeline kneeled next to the calf. "You aren't planning on sending this thing home with me, are you?"

Jackson widened his eyes and pointed to his chest. "Me, do that to you?"

"Yeah, you're going to do that to me." She pulled off her city-girl gloves and stroked the calf's back. "Where would I put a calf?"

"You have an empty barn and a corral."

The sucking air sound meant an empty bottle. Jade pulled the bottle from the calf's mouth and it chased after her, butting against her, wanting more. She laughed and stuck out her fingers. The calf brought his long tongue around her hand.

"What do we do now?" Jade kneeled in front of the little bull calf.

"For now we'll put him in a stall with plenty of straw to sleep on and feed him again later."

"He'll be all alone." Madeline stroked the calf and looked at him with kind of pleading, kind of accusing eyes. Great, an orphaned calf and two big-hearted females.

"Yes, he will. But that's about the only option. He wouldn't survive on his own in the pasture." He picked up the calf and headed toward an empty stall, trying to figure out a way to undo the sad look in Madeline's eyes. It hadn't been but a couple of weeks ago that he'd just do what he had to do and that would have been the end of it.

A female around the place changed everything. They brought emotion into farming. He sighed and shook his head because now he couldn't walk away without it bugging him, too.

He put the calf in the stall and turned, smiling because he was going to be the hero. "I'll get a goat to keep him company."

"A goat?"

"Yeah, Ryder Johnson has a few goats that he sometimes pairs up with foals. We'll stop by there on our way back from the Mad Cow."

Jade leaned in, looking at the bawling, unhappy calf. "Can't we get him a friend now?"

He shook his head and pulled out his phone. "Let me call Ryder."

He made the call and fifteen minutes later Ryder pulled up to the barn and led a big, fat goat into Jackson's barn. Ryder grinned, tipped his hat and handed the lead rope of the goat to Jade.

"Told you to buy a goat." He shot the comment at Jackson.

"Right, I should have listened to you." Jackson opened the stall door and the goat walked right in, eyed her new companion in unblinking silence and grabbed a mouthful of straw.

The calf stopped crying as the goat moved closer.

"Perfect." Madeline smiled and watched as the calf followed the goat around the stall. Jackson shook his head. It was that easy to make her smile.

And he'd never cared more about making a woman happy. That thought made him want to jump in his truck and drive far and fast from this situation and this moment. Realizations like that one didn't come around very often.

It had never happened to him before.

"Now, can we go to lunch?" He slipped a convincing arm around her waist and moved her toward the door. Ryder walked on out but turned as they followed.

"Let me know if you need anything else." Ryder grinned. "Like advice."

"I doubt I need advice from you." Jackson glared and Ryder didn't seem to notice.

"Of course not. I mean, why would you need advice? You've been ranching all your life."

"Exactly. I'm very good at ranching."

And they both knew they weren't talking about ranching. Madeline walked away, fortunately not getting it. She followed Jade to the fence and one of the horses walked up to let them rub her neck.

"Nothing changes a man like a good woman and a kid."

Ryder pushed his hat down on his head a little tighter.

"I haven't changed." Jackson didn't have a woman or a kid, not really. He watched them walk down the

Holiday Blessing

bugged him, that Jade wasn't
t his.

the twins are ransacking the
hey're chewing and dragging

nas for you all."

a later, Jackson. I think your
different than you expected,

greed, but he knew that the
s he'd had about Jade having
s. He wondered if she'd have
her mother.

ried to tell himself it wasn't
d it cut deep, thinking about

l shrill. Madeline and Jade
ction. "Let's get some lunch."
ne truck together. Madeline in
de did that on purpose every

Chapter Thirteen

The Mad Cow Diner looked like Christmas come early. Madeline walked in next to Jackson and Jade. She tried to pretend she went to lunch with someone like Jackson every day. But the stares from the locals reminded her that she couldn't fool them or herself. She'd been here a year and she'd never dated. When well-meaning friends tried to match her up with a nice guy, she always said a polite "No, thank you."

She stared at the Christmas tree and decorations, trying to ignore the heat creeping up her neck. Jade grabbed her hand and pulled her toward a nativity, hand-carved by a local artist. The tree sparkled with clear lights and Christmas music played softly on hidden speakers.

Last year she'd been in town just a few months and she'd joined Vera for Christmas at the Mad Cow. Vera always had a big meal for folks in town without family. Madeline had received the same invitation for this year.

Vera walked out of the kitchen, wiping her hands on her apron. She grinned big when she saw them. "Well, Merry Christmas."

Madeline smiled back. Vera had switched from her

normal blue dress to a red dress, white apron and a Santa hat.

"Merry Christmas, Vera." Madeline accepted the other woman's warm hug and skittered a look sideways to find Jackson heading their way.

"Isn't that nativity beautiful?" Vera put an arm around Jade. "A man in our church carved that for me. I love the look of love on Mary's face. She'd just had the most perfect baby in the world, and she had to wonder why God had brought this moment to her. I always wonder how she felt, being so young and being put in that situation. I think she must have felt as awed as the shepherds."

"I think the cows were awed, too." Jade grinned as she looked at the scene. "We have a calf."

"Do we?" Vera's brows arched and she turned to look at Jackson.

He shrugged and let it go. But Vera didn't. Her gaze shot up and she smiled. "Why, Jackson Cooper, look at that, Madeline is under the mistletoe."

"Vera." Madeline tried to step away.

Jackson caught her hand, a wicked grin on his face. He smiled at Vera and then at her again. His hand on hers was rough and warm. "We can't ignore mistletoe. Vera would be crushed."

"I would indeed." Vera smiled big. "I move it every morning because I want to keep things interesting."

"But—" Madeline looked around the restaurant, half-full and everyone staring at them. A table of women giggled and pointed.

Jackson grinned and her heart stopped protesting. She stopped wanting to escape. How did he do that? When he stepped close she wobbled a little and he slid a hand to her back, steadying her. "One little kiss won't hurt."

She nodded but wanted to disagree. It could hurt, very much. He leaned and dropped the sweetest of kisses on her mouth. When he pulled back, his smile had faded.

"Maddie, I'm all out of self-control. Good Jackson has left the building."

Vera laughed. "From the look on her face, I think Good Maddie has left the building, too."

Madeline shook her head. "I'm very much still here."

Vera clucked a little and moved them in the direction of a corner booth, out of view. She said, "I think what the two of you need is a nice bowl of chicken and dumplings. Weather like we're having calls for comfort food. The weatherman said today that we've had two weeks of below normal temperatures."

"Chicken and dumplings do sound good, Vera." Jackson's hand remained on Madeline's back and he reached for Jade who had stopped to look at Christmas cards taped to the wall. "This way, kiddo."

As they walked people were talking behind their hands and nodding in their direction. Madeline pulled her jacket a little tighter around herself and blinked fast to clear her vision. Why did moments like this make her want to hide again?

Being stared at, whispered about. It had all been too much a part of her life all those years ago. Being interviewed by police, going before judges and lawyers, facing her mother that last time. Her heart squeezed tight.

A hand touched her arm, guiding her to the booth and into a seat. She scooted across the bench and took

ow, sighing with relief when

do for the rest of the after-

m her menu when Jackson

eated next to her, grinned.

e arena. This weather isn't

s gaze settled on Madeline

ver. He didn't look away for

used on the menu, unable to

yes.

shopping?" He smiled up at

vith an order pad.

and then Jackson returned

n, pulling them back to the

g?" He picked up the wrap-

ned it into a paper wad that

the nose. "I'm kind of an

omen. It comes from having

unds fun." Madeline stirred

coffee that Vera was famous

ve." Jackson reached for the

early emptied into her iced

didn't laugh. "I have to go

here for Christmas."

ad and waited for Jackson's

e for Jade who just wanted a

"Jade, I'm not going to leave you on your own. I promise."

Jade shrugged her slim shoulders like it didn't matter. But it did matter. It mattered more than any of them could say. To a girl who had nothing, not even family, it mattered.

"You don't even think you're my dad."

Jackson leaned forward, resting his arms on the table. "What do you mean by that?"

"Why else would you need a DNA test?" Jade fiddled with her napkin, tearing it into little pieces. "You're looking for a way to skip out on me."

"I'm not." He tossed his hat on the bench and brushed a hand through his hair. "Jade, I'm a bachelor. I've been single and on my own for a long time. I'm not going to know how to make 'dad' decisions right off the bat."

"Right, yeah, whatever." Jade hunkered, her shoulders curved forward and her head down. "I'll be okay."

"Jade, you'll be more than okay. I promise."

The waitress appeared with their chicken and dumplings, as well as a big basket of rolls and salads for the three of them.

"Let's eat and have a good day. Tomorrow we'll figure something out."

Jade nodded but she wouldn't look up, wouldn't make eye contact with either of them. She blew on a steaming bite of chicken and dumplings but didn't take the bite. Instead she looked down at the bowl, tears dripping down her cheeks. Madeline touched her hand and smiled when Jade looked up at her.

"It'll be okay. I know people have told you that before, but Jackson isn't going to let anything happen to you. He's going to be there for you."

And then Madeline looked at Jackson, pleading without words for him to keep the promise she'd just made for him. He had to be the person this little girl needed. Someone had to be there for Jade.

Two hours later Jackson still couldn't shake the way Madeline's words back at the Mad Cow had shaken him. Jackson in Charge wasn't the name of this little family drama. The only person Jackson really knew how to take care of was Jackson.

Somehow, though, a kid and a woman had become a big part of his life. He walked behind them as they browsed the second flea market of the day. They were looking at fancy little tea cups that wouldn't hold more than a thimble of liquid. While they looked at tea cups he tried to remember who he had been a week ago.

"This one is pretty." Jade picked up a cup and handed it to Madeline who held it up to the light and examined it.

The guy gene didn't allow him to see a thing different about that cup. It looked like every other cup they'd looked at.

"It's beautiful." Madeline turned to him, big smile, eyes dark and pulling him in. He was about to tell her he agreed.

He couldn't stop himself.

"It is pretty." He blinked because he didn't drink tea. He didn't shop in flea markets for old tea cups that other people had been drinking out of for years.

She laughed and he knew he'd blown it. "You're not good at this."

"Sorry, I'm not a tea person. Or a cup person."

"Or a flea market person." Madeline put the cup

back on the shelf. "We should go to a store with guy stuff. Fishing poles and guns."

"Madeline, do you want that cup?"

She shook her head. "Even I wouldn't spend that much for a cup. Let's go, before you break out in hives."

How far gone was a guy when he picked up the flowery tea cup and carried it to the counter? As he paid he told himself this was going to pass. But watching the delight on Madeline's face when he handed her that bag holding the perfect tea cup, he wasn't quite sure. He wondered if he needed to go back and buy another dozen of those cups, because if each one put a smile on her face, it was worth it.

She led him out of the store by the hand, Jade skipping ahead of them.

"What am I going to do?" He watched the girl walk ahead of them, window shopping.

"Tell her the truth." Matter of fact Madeline.

"Yeah, sounds easy, doesn't it?"

"It won't be. She wants to be a Cooper. And who could blame her. She wants you for a dad. Any little girl would."

That did more than surprise him. He stopped walking, but kept his eye on the teenager a short distance ahead of them. Okay, he couldn't let it go. He turned to look at Madeline.

"Why in the world would a kid want me for a dad?"

"Really?" Madeline watched Jade, too. "You don't get that? You have everything to offer. You're a good man with a wonderful home and a family. You can take care of her, make her feel safe."

"Keep talking, you're starting to convince me." He grinned down at Madeline and she turned away, cheeks

'd think so highly of

king for a young girl
table home."
I'm not dad material.
decent job at taking
ortant fact is the one

ng she has to one."
out that?" He was the
dad. That didn't say
wasn't anyone's dad.
be there for her.
walked away from.
a with a waitress who
nt dinner and empty
ected someone to be

xt to him, believing
led softly and shook
same thing, someone

re?" Jade turned from
em, sliding a little on

thought came to him,
could let her believe

d headed up the side-
. "See anything you

I thought we could go
homemade jewelry."

"Let's go." He opened the door for the two women to walk in ahead of him.

It looked like trouble to Jackson. A jewelry store plus two females equaled serious trouble any way he looked at it. Not that he hadn't given women jewelry before. For Christmas. To say goodbye. Once, a long time ago he'd bought a promise ring for a girl in school. After another month of dating he realized forever felt like, well, forever. He'd taken the ring back and her brother had knocked him almost into eternity.

His phone rang, saving him from the ohhing and ahhing as Jade and Madeline went from display cabinet to display cabinet. Saved by the bell, he walked outside to take the call.

"Jackson Cooper, bring my daughter back." The voice on the other end didn't sound at all familiar. The words slurred and mumbled, forcing him to plug his opposite ear.

"I can't hear you."

"This is Gloria. Bring my daughter back. She's not your kid."

"So you did get the messages I left." He walked a short distance away from the front of the jewelry store. "Listen, Gloria, I can't really talk right now. I'm bringing her back tomorrow. But we're going to discuss this situation."

"We aren't going to discuss anything. She's my kid and I could have you arrested."

Anger shot through him, white hot and making his heart beat hard in this neck. He swallowed a lot of things he knew he shouldn't say in favor of carefully chosen words.

"Don't worry, the police know that I have her. My

question to you is, why didn't you call sooner? Why didn't you file a missing persons report?"

"That's none of your business. Jade knows how to take care of herself."

The anger took a pivotal turn for the worse and he had to stand there for a long minute, finding a way to respond without making the situation worse. "Gloria, she's thirteen."

Gloria laughed, loud and harsh. "Right, and you care?"

"Yeah, I care."

"Just bring her home."

The phone went dead. Jackson stood with the cell phone in his hand watching the steady stream of traffic down the street. A hand touched his arm. He turned and Madeline gave him a cautious look.

"Problem?"

He shook his head and pocketed his phone. "Nothing I can't handle. Let's go back inside and see if Jade found something wonderful she can't live without."

"She found several items that fit that description."

"What about you?"

"No, I'm not a jewelry person. And as interesting as their jewelry is, I'm more of an antiques girl. There's something about owning something that someone treasured for years, or generations."

"Gotcha." He touched her back with one hand and reached to push the door open with the other. Antiques. He filed that away for future reference.

The whirlwind of a teenager grabbed him and for the next fifteen minutes pointed out every awesome thing she could find. And then she told him she didn't want anything. She was happy just to look. Jackson hugged her tight. If he'd had a kid, he'd want her to be just like this one. He'd want her to be wild about living life, meeting people and experiencing new things.

He bought her a matching set of jewelry and she threw her arms around his neck and whispered, "I love you, Dad."

Over her shoulder he caught Madeline's soft-hearted expression, eyes filling with unshed tears. "You're welcome, kiddo."

She deserved a dad. Tomorrow he would have to tell her the truth. He knew, from talking to Gloria, that if he didn't, Gloria would. It would hurt less coming from him. Nothing in the world would keep it from hurting, though.

"We should probably head home." He paid for the jewelry and handed the bag, all decorated in bows and swirls, to Jade.

Madeline stood next to the door waiting for them. "Good idea. I have to be at practice in two hours and I bet that puppy is going crazy wanting outside. And that's your fault, Jackson Cooper."

"My fault?" He opened the door for them. "What, exactly, is my fault?"

"The puppy at my house making who knows what kind of mess."

"Oh yeah, the puppy. Okay, that probably is a little bit my fault."

"So you'll come over and clean up her puppy messes?"

"Nope, but I'll buy you dinner tomorrow evening." Jackson gave her his best smile because he couldn't take a chance that she'd say no.

"Tomorrow? But you'll be in Oklahoma City." Her eyes widened and her chin came up a slight notch as she got what he meant.

» with us."

iet as Jade moved ahead of

of a store that held a display

»esn't she?" Madeline slowed

tched his to hers.

Gloria is pretty determined.

»me and she pointed out that

the birth certificate."

proves otherwise."

couldn't look Madeline in

e end. Jade had to go home.

nis life. Everything would go

»ack to his life. They'd each

lives. Whatever lesson he'd

uld be over.

urt like crazy to think about

ld be his own again. No, he

rty anytime soon.

Chapter Fourteen

A quiet house. Madeline walked through her front door after work on Friday and thought about how this quiet used to be normal. No Jade. No Angel the puppy. Heather Cooper was babysitting the dog for her until they got back from taking Jade to Oklahoma City. No noise and no clutter.

After today her life was her own again. No more Jackson Cooper messing around in her business, or her emotions. She should sigh a sigh of relief over that one. Good riddance!

She dropped her bag by the hall tree and kicked off her boots. But she didn't have a lot of time. Jackson wanted to leave for Oklahoma City in an hour. That meant packing an overnight bag, changing clothes and tidying up a little before he got there to pick her up.

The plan included them staying one night in Oklahoma City. She would stay in a separate hotel room with Jade, to keep the girl safe and watch her. Tomorrow morning they would take Jade to her mother. And then they'd head home. Alone.

End of story. End of this little chapter in her life. This very complicated, cluttered chapter. As she walked through the hall the phone rang. She ignored it. It quit ringing but immediately started again. Madeline reached for it as she headed to her room to grab extra clothes.

"Hello."

"Madeline, it's me. It's your mother."

Madeline cringed and then she groaned. "Stop calling me."

"It's almost Christmas. I just wondered if maybe you would reconsider seeing me. Please. If you would just see me, just once?"

"Do you know what happened to Sara?" Madeline grabbed jeans out of her closet and two sweaters. She shoved pajamas into her bag and extra warm socks.

A long pause and then her mother spoke again. "Honey, I'm sorry."

"Sorry? I think we've established that. You're sorry and you want to be forgiven." Madeline leaned against the wall and closed her eyes. And as much as she fought the urge to stay angry, to stay bitter, she wanted to forgive. The little girl in her cried out for her mother.

Over the years, every now and then, she'd thought about what it would be like if her mother came back. If her mother could be the person she wanted her to be, needed her to be. That dream had seemed far better than the thought of always being alone with no family to turn to.

"Madeline, Sara..." Across the line Madeline heard a sniffle and then a sob. "Honey, she killed herself the night that she took you to town. She wanted you safe, I think. She did what I should have done."

Madeline walked to the window and looked out at the barren December landscape painted in shades of brown and gray. Bleak. Winter was always so bleak.

This moment felt like winter. It ached deep down inside, frozen and cold.

"I have to get off the phone now." Madeline held the phone to her ear as she slipped into jeans.

"Maybe before Christmas we can talk again?"

Madeline nodded even though the woman on the other end couldn't see. "I'll pray about it."

"Thank you. Oh, Madeline, thank you."

The call ended. Madeline sat on the edge of the bed and thought about the girl who hadn't really been her sister. Sara hadn't saved herself. She had given up. And no one had ever told Madeline. They'd allowed her to search, to ask questions, and they'd hidden the truth from her.

Maybe she could have found the truth if she'd tried a little harder? The one thing she couldn't have done was save Sara.

A car honked. She shoved her makeup bag and extra clothes into an overnight bag, slid her feet into boots and jerked her coat off the hall tree on her way out the door.

Jade jumped out of the truck and motioned for Madeline to climb in. Always pushing her into the middle. Madeline shook her head and climbed in. Jackson smiled big as she slid across the leather seat. He tipped his hat a little and winked. As she slid close she realized how good he smelled. And how good it felt to sit next to him.

The door slammed and Jade reached for her seatbelt. She didn't smile, though. Instead she watched out the window, shoulders slumped. Madeline touched her arm and Jade turned, smiling just a little.

"It'll be okay."

Jade shrugged. "Yeah, sure it will."

"We're not walking out of your life, Jade." Jackson shifted gears, his hand brushing Madeline's knee. She scooted a little closer to Jade.

"Right, I know." Jade looked out the window again, ignoring them.

Were they so different, she and Jade? Madeline thought not. Both had mothers they wanted to escape from. Madeline had escaped once and then she'd had to escape again. And again. She wasn't going to run anymore. This time she would face her mother. She'd been learning that facing fears sometimes meant overcoming them, seeing them for the tiny ant hills they were rather than the mountains they appeared to be.

Maybe her mother would be another mountain conquered.

Maybe someday Jade would conquer her mountains, her giants. It took faith, learning to rely on faith.

A hand touched Madeline's. She turned her attention from Jade to the man sitting next to her. Jackson Cooper. Her fears had changed from how he could hurt her, to how he could break her heart.

She hadn't expected that.

"How was your day?" He slid a quick look her way before turning his attention back to the road.

"Good day at school. My mother called again." She meant to be strong but her voice broke a little. Jackson shot her another quick look.

"You okay?"

"Good. I'm good." An easy smile to prove the point.

"Are we going to stop and eat?" Jade turned from the window to ask the question. "Are you taking me home as soon as we get to Oklahoma City?"

"We will eat. I do need to check in with your mom as soon as we get to town, but I thought you could stay with us tonight. I reserved two rooms, one for the two of you and one for me."

"Cool, a hotel. The only hotel I've ever stayed in was the shelter when Mom…" Jade's words faded off and she turned her attention back to the window. "How come you had to bring bulls?"

Madeline glanced back at the trailer hooked to the truck.

"I'm selling them." Jackson looked in the rearview mirror. "We'll stop at a ranch outside of the city, unload the cattle and drop the trailer. I'll pick the trailer up on our way back home."

"*Your* way back home." Jade corrected with a big frown.

"Jade, this isn't goodbye."

"Yeah, I know." She reached to turn up the radio. "Silent Night" filled the cab of the truck.

Madeline started singing. Jackson glanced at her, a quick look at her profile. Jade kept staring out the window for a minute but then she couldn't help herself. He figured that's what Madeline intended. Pretty soon Jade and Madeline were both singing. An elbow jabbed his gut.

"Broken ribs, remember?" He grunted and grimaced a little.

"Sing." Madeline smiled up at him, innocent and sweet.

He hadn't sung "Silent Night" in years but he joined them for the chorus. The chorus went high. They laughed at him.

"Hey, you said to sing."

"We changed our minds." Jade looked pained and stuck her fingers in her ears. "Please don't sing again."

"Give me another chance." He cranked the volume to

George Strait singing a Christmas song. "This is more like it."

Madeline openly laughed. "You're not even going to tell us that you compare to George Strait."

He winked and grinned at her. "I'm a cowboy. I have jeans and a…cute grin."

"You're full of yourself." She shook her head and started singing.

For the next two hours they sang to the radio. Jade finally fell asleep. He didn't know if Madeline had intended for it to be such a great distraction, but it had worked. He owed her.

Jackson slowed the truck for the turn that would take them to the small town where he had a buyer for the bull calves in the trailer.

"Are we almost there?" Jade blinked a few times and then rubbed the sleep from her eyes.

"Almost." Jackson took the next right. The trailer lurched and the truck pulled a little. "We'll eat after we drop these calves."

"I'm starving." Jade again. She stretched and then leaned her head on Madeline.

He pulled up the driveway, dialed his phone and listened to the man on the other end give directions on which gate to back up to with the trailer.

"Give me fifteen minutes. The two of you can stay in here where it's warm."

Madeline nodded and watched him get out of the truck. He looked back in at her. Lately he'd wondered a lot what she thought about him. If he had any sense at all he wouldn't want an answer to that question.

Thirty minutes later Jackson was back in the truck and they were on the road. He cranked the heat and tossed his gloves in the floor of the truck. "Man, it's freezing out there."

"Is that sleet?" Madeline nodded, indicating moisture hitting the windshield.

"Yeah, I think it is. And maybe freezing rain. We need to get to Oklahoma City." He glanced at his watch. "I wonder if it's doing this in Tulsa."

His parents and brother were in Tulsa heading up a charity bull riding event for Travis's favorite charity, a group home for children taken from their parents. Kids like Jade. Hopefully the weather didn't mean the event got cancelled.

The frozen stuff hit the windshield. He flipped on his wipers and turned the heat to defrost. They were driving through Oklahoma City and already cars were sliding off into the ditch. Good thing he'd left that stock trailer behind. He'd pick it up on his way home.

"Can we eat now?"

Jackson shook his head. "No, we're going to see your mom first. And then we'll head for our hotel and order from room service."

Out of the corner of his eye he saw Jade wringing her hands and biting her lip.

"Jade…" He stopped because he wouldn't tell her again that it would be okay. She'd heard it enough. He didn't know what would happen, so how could he make promises?

The GPS gave directions to the address Jade's mom had given him. It was dark and the houses were dark. People stood on porches, walked out to cars. Houses were boarded up and looked empty. The house they stopped in front of didn't look much better than the abandoned houses.

"Home sweet home." Jade opened her door and got out.

The freezing rain had stopped but it was still cold. Jackson slid a little as he got out. He reached back in for Madeline. Jade had already headed up the sidewalk.

Gloria, not the Gloria he remembered from years ago, but a thinner version with stringy hair and a gaunt face, stepped outside. She shivered in her thin T-shirt and skin-tight jeans.

"Did you tell her you're not her dad?"

Jackson shot Jade a look, saw her face pale, her eyes widen.

"Not like this, Gloria."

"Well, she's got to stop living in a fantasy world, thinking she's some princess who got lost. This is it, sweetheart, home sweet home."

"Gloria, stop." Jackson rushed up the steps, reaching for Jade as the girl bolted.

"You should have told me." Jade slipped from his grasp and ran down the steps, down the sidewalk. At the street she turned. "I thought I could trust you."

"Jade, you can." But how could she trust anyone? "Come back and talk."

When he realized she didn't plan on talking, he went after her. But she was gone. She disappeared into the dark night. Madeline ran to his side, yelling for Jade to come back. They walked down the street together, past houses with loud music cranked. People shouted and cars honked.

"Where'd she go?" Madeline shivered next to him.

"It's hard to tell. Maybe she has a friend around here somewhere. Maybe Gloria knows."

They walked back to the house. Gloria had gone inside.

"How does this happen?" Madeline asked as they walked to the front door. "How does a life get this out of control?"

"Wrong choices build up." Jackson shrugged and slid an arm around the shivering woman who didn't have to be here with him. "So, your mom called again?"

"She wants to see me. I'm thinking I might. I don't know. She told me that Sara killed herself."

Jackson pulled her close to his side. "I'm sorry."

She nodded and reached to knock on the door. "The important thing now is finding Jade."

Gloria opened the door. In the light from the living room her skin looked yellow and dry. She scowled at them as if she couldn't remember who they were or why they were there.

"What?"

"We didn't find Jade." Jackson pushed the door open. "Mind if we come in?"

"I'd rather you not."

"Right, but we are." He led Madeline into the smoke-filled living room. It stank of old food, cigarettes and unchanged cat litter. "Where do you think she went?"

"What do you care? You're not her dad." Gloria plopped down on the sofa and lit another cigarette.

"My name is on her birth certificate. You did that."

She shrugged. "Yeah, well, I couldn't think of anyone else to put on there. I wanted her to have a dad. You seemed decent."

"Did you think I was her dad, Gloria?"

"No, not really. I just thought if something ever happened to me, you'd be contacted and the kind of family you came from, you wouldn't leave a kid on her own."

He tensed and shoved his hands into his pockets. He'd never wanted to hurt a woman, not once in his life.

ty close to that point. "Where

eacher's house. Maybe at a
e home tomorrow. Once she
her little vacation is over."

her at all?" Madeline's voice
ed for her hand. "She's a child.

Madeline's face, the whites of
skin. "Don't come in here and
aughter, Princess. Yeah, you're
who ain't never had to suffer."
at you're talking about." Mad-
o know that Jade deserves for

iloria dropped back to her seat
them away. "You take her."
stepped closer. He kneeled to
not before he saw tears streak-
epatitis. But it doesn't matter.
nning away every time some-
oesn't like. You're not her dad,
oirth certificate. Take her with
nily or something."

hand and then lit another ciga-

have somewhere I need to be."
es and grabbed a jacket off the
n't know where she is. Come
be she'll be here."

tarted to walk away Jackson
noring the marks on her arms.
he person he'd met fourteen

years ago. A young woman and her sister traveling and having adventures.

"What about Jade?"

Gloria laughed, a croaking sound that ended in a cough. "Take her, Jackson. I don't want her. Give her to your girlfriend. Take her to your family. Or call the police and have them pick her up. I've had a good time not worrying about her."

"Really?" Madeline stepped between Gloria and the door. "Is that really how you feel about your daughter?"

Gloria stopped to grab a beat-up, dirty purse. "Get out of my house."

"No, I want to know if that's how you really feel about your child." Madeline shook so hard Jackson didn't know if she'd stay on her feet or fall over. But she didn't appear to be about to back down. She had the look of a mother tiger about to do battle for her cub and he wanted to hug her.

"Look around you." Gloria swung a thin arm around the dirty living room. "This is it. This is all I have. One more mouth to feed. That's what Jade is. She needs stuff. She's always wanting new clothes. She wants to go places."

"You'll sign over custody?" Jackson stepped close to Madeline. "I'll get a lawyer tomorrow and have something temporary drawn up."

"Yeah, sure." Gloria's eyes glistened. "I'll sign."

Jackson pulled out his wallet. "Take this."

"You buying my kid, Jackson?"

"No, Gloria, I'm helping out someone who used to be a friend."

Gloria motioned them out of her house without saying anything and then she walked down the side-

he front porch, unsure of how
happened.

He glanced down at Madeline.

ea where to start. Somewhere
rk houses, a few with a sprin-
s or a tree showing through a
refuge. She was hiding from
her down.

his hand. "We'll find her."

Chapter Fifteen

They didn't find her. Madeline woke up the next morning with the sun peeking through the heavy curtains of the hotel and an empty feeling in the region of her heart. They'd driven for hours. They'd stopped and asked people on the street if they'd seen a young girl. They'd called the local police for help.

Jade had disappeared. Madeline looked at the other bed, still made. Jade should have been in that bed. She should have been safe, knowing that Jackson loved her the way a father loved a daughter.

That thought did fill Madeline's heart. It filled up empty spaces, that Jackson could love Jade that way, in a way that would make a girl like Jade feel safe, secure, not afraid. If only Jade knew.

Madeline forced herself to get up and get ready for another day. She prayed, the way they'd stopped and prayed last night, she and Jackson, that they'd find Jade safe. She closed her eyes thinking of that moment that Jackson had reached for her hand and said they'd forgotten something.

How could they have forgotten to pray?

She opened her eyes and looked in the mirror. She

prayed again, but this time for herself, not for Jade. Her heart had moved into foreign and very dangerous territory. Her heart, crazy, inexperienced organ that it was, wanted to run away with emotions that were new.

Someone pounded on her door. She peeked through the peephole and saw Jackson standing in the hall. He had his hat in his hands and he was looking up, waiting. She pulled the door open.

"Any news?"

He shook his head. "None. Let's grab some breakfast and we'll see if we can find her."

Madeline looked back into her room. "Should I pack my stuff?"

"No, I already reserved the rooms for a second night. If we find Jade, we can go home, but if we don't, we have a place to come back to."

"We'll find her." She grabbed her purse and coat and pulled the door closed behind her. "She's hurt and she's running but she'll be back."

Hurt and running were two things Madeline knew from experience.

Outside the hotel it was difficult to tell that there were any problems in the world. They'd stayed in a quaint section of Oklahoma City called Bricktown. Arriving late last night Madeline had seen the twinkling of Christmas lights and heard music, but neither of them had been in the mood to enjoy the city.

They'd gotten a cup of coffee and headed to their individual rooms. Now, Bricktown surrounded them. Bricktown, once a warehouse district, a place where industry thrived, had been reinvented, and turned into an entertainment district with restaurants and other attractions.

They walked along the canal, watching steam rise from the water. Neither talked for a long time.

"We should eat something." Jackson led her toward a restaurant that appeared to be open. "I could use coffee."

"That sounds good." Madeline walked through the door he opened for her.

Weeks ago she would have looked down, avoided touching him as she walked through the door of the Mad Cow. Today she looked up, smiled and hoped he'd return the gesture. She wanted to comfort him, to reassure him.

The door eased closed. Jackson leaned, touching his forehead to hers. "Thank you."

She nodded, still close to him, unable to move away. "You're welcome."

"What am I going to do with a kid?" He laughed a little and then pulled back from her. "What was I thinking?"

"You were thinking that Jade needs a family and you can give her a wonderful family."

The hostess led them to a table. When they were seated Jackson reached for her hands. "I'm not a family. I'm me. I'm a single, almost thirty-four-year-old man who has never had a relationship that lasted longer than two months. To be honest, Madeline, you're about the best relationship I've ever had."

"That's not promising, is it?" She pulled her hands from his and reached for the menu, a laminated card stuck between the sugar bowl and the napkin holder.

"I think it is." He nodded at the waitress when she brought a pot of coffee to their table.

Madeline smiled up at the waitress. "I'll take biscuits and gravy."

Jackson ordered the same. "I called a lawyer this morning. He's a friend of my brother Blake's and he lives here in Oklahoma City. He's writing something up for us and he's going to meet us at Gloria's."

"That's good. I only wish we could find Jade and tell her."

"We're going to find her. I'm not leaving here without her."

After they'd finished eating, they walked the block to the parking garage. Jackson spent part of the time talking on the phone, first to his parents, then the police and then the lawyer. Finally he slid the phone into his pocket and Madeline asked the question that had been on her mind since the previous day.

"Jackson, from the very beginning, you seemed to know that Jade wasn't yours."

He pulled out his truck key and kept walking. Madeline had to pick up her pace to keep up. He had her door open and she stopped, waiting for him to answer. He helped her in the truck and then he stood in the open door.

"I knew she wasn't mine because I can't have kids." He closed the door and walked away.

Madeline leaned back in the seat, closing her eyes against the pain she'd seen in his eyes. When he got in next to her she opened her eyes and looked at him. He started the truck and shifted into Reverse without speaking.

"I'm sorry. It's none of my business."

"No, it isn't. But now you know. She isn't mine. It was never possible. I had a bad case of the mumps as a kid…" His voice trailed off and he focused on driving.

"But you didn't tell her. You allowed her to stay."

Jackson sighed and yanked off his hat. He tossed

it on the seat between them and he didn't look at her. Madeline reached, touching her fingers to his. He moved his hand so that their fingers laced together.

"Madeline, I let her stay because I thought 'what if?' And I let her stay because she was a kid who wanted a family bad enough she was willing to hitch a ride and forge a note to find one. I also didn't want her taken into custody, not at Christmas."

"So am I the only one who knows your secret?"

"That I can't have kids? My family knows."

She shook her head. "No, I mean the other secret. The part about you being one of the most decent men in Dawson."

"You've forgotten that I'm the Jackson that dates a different woman every week. I'm the guy who keeps my mother and grandmother on their knees praying I'll come back to church."

"Right, you're that Jackson." But he wasn't that Jackson at all. Not anymore.

He glanced at her and laughed. "Don't get that look in your eyes like you've discovered something wonderful and noble about me, or some secret that explains my wicked ways. I am who I am, Madeline."

They finished the drive to Gloria's in silence. Madeline didn't need to ask for further explanations. Jackson was who he was. Note to self: don't get attached to a cowboy who breaks hearts for a hobby. Even when that cowboy is noble to the core.

Jade was sitting on the front porch of her mother's house. Jackson pulled up and a big, dark blue sedan pulled up right behind him. That would be the lawyer and his wife, the notary. As Jackson got out of the truck, Jade walked into the house, ignoring him.

Madeline was ignoring him, too. That was for the best. She was tea. He was coffee. She would someday want to get married and have babies. He could picture her in a little house, a baby in her arms, some nice guy coming home from his office job.

He wanted to hurt that nice guy with the office job. But right now wasn't the time to be plotting against fictional people in Madeline's life. Now he had to deal with Jade. That had to be his focus.

"George, do you have the paper?" Jackson held his hand out, shook the hand of the lawyer and then took the paper he handed over.

"Right here. Are you sure about this?"

"Yeah, I'm sure. I've never been more sure about anything." Almost anything. Madeline stood a short distance away. When he smiled at her she looked away.

Gloria opened the front door of her house and dragged her daughter out. Jade jerked away from her mother. She stood on the porch, still wearing the clothes she'd worn the day before. Today, though, her look of defiance had multiplied. She seemed to be daring all of them to speak to her.

Madeline didn't seem to care what Jade's look said. She walked right up the steps and gathered the girl into her arms. She whispered and Jade shot him a look. Her eyes got big, watered, and her nose turned pink.

What in the world was he thinking?

"Jade, do you want to go home with me?" He handed the paper to Gloria. "Sign this."

She jerked it from his hand and looked it over. "Fine, give me a pen and get her out of here."

Her words were cold, callous. Jackson didn't know if Jade noticed, but her mother's eyes didn't reflect that tone. Her eyes watered and she had to look away, to brush the tears from her cheeks.

Gloria signed the paper. Jackson signed it. The lawyer signed it. Jackson turned to Jade. "Hug your mother."

"She isn't my mother."

Madeline gasped and Jackson shot her a look. He didn't need another emotional female in this mix. He turned to Jade, now officially in his custody. "Hug your mother."

Jade had walked off the porch but she stomped back up the steps and she hugged Gloria. Gloria held her tight for a minute and then let her go quick. She stepped back and looked away. "You go with Jackson and try to behave. I want you to visit."

"She'll visit." Jackson didn't know what to do now. This time he let Madeline handle it. She hugged Gloria and gave her a phone number. In case she needed anything.

They were walking down the sidewalk when Gloria ran down and grabbed Jade again. She held her daughter tight and then whispered, "I did my best. I'm sorry."

Jade stared at her mother, unsure. "I know. Thank you for letting me go with Jackson."

"Yeah, okay." And then Gloria ran back up the steps and into the house.

"Let's go home." Jackson opened the door. Madeline climbed in last this time. She put Jade between them and he figured that said it all.

On the drive home he had plenty of time to think about the situation he'd put himself in. Jade slept next to him, her head resting on Madeline's shoulder. Madeline had fallen asleep as well.

He turned the radio on low but he didn't hear the music. He had too much to think about. Like what in the world would he do with a teenager? He didn't want to dump Jade on his parents. He'd take her to his sister Heather and then figure out a plan. He guessed he'd need a live-in housekeeper. He'd also have to put her in school as soon as possible.

When he stopped to pick up the trailer, Madeline woke up.

"I guess we're not home?"

He shook his head. "Just an hour out of the city."

By the time he got back in the truck she had fallen back to sleep. He looked at her, sleeping like that, and he wondered what it would be like, to have a life with a woman like Madeline. A man would be blessed to have her as a wife.

He wanted to be that man.

In thirty-three years he'd never had that thought. Not this way, in a way that settled in his gut, twisted him up inside. Yeah, there had been women, most of them not exactly the kind he'd take home to his mother, that he'd dreamed about marrying.

This woman, though, she'd gotten under his skin. He could see her raising a bunch of kids, growing old with a guy, having grandchildren.

Children and grandchildren. He knew someday she'd have those things. She'd have everything she deserved. But not with him.

She'd get married. He'd stay in his old farmhouse, raising Jade, sometimes dating. Maybe he wouldn't date. That game was getting old, as old as he was.

He drove through Dawson, one main street, convenience store, feed store, Vera's. He waved as a neighboring farmer walked out of the feed store. At the edge of town he turned on the paved county road that led to Cooper property, and Madeline's little house in the middle of the vast acreage that belonged to his family.

"Madeline, we're almost there."

She woke up, blinked a few times and rubbed sleep from her eyes. "Wow, I slept the entire way?"

"We had a rough day yesterday. You needed the sleep."

When he pulled in her driveway, she gathered up her purse and overnight bag. "I would walk you to the door, but I'd better get her home."

"That's okay, I'm a big girl." She smiled at him, a sweet as honey smile. "Goodbye, Jackson."

He tipped his hat and smiled. "Goodbye, Madeline."

She had already jumped out of the truck and was going up the sidewalk to her front door. She stopped on the porch and waved.

Goodbye, Madeline. As she drove to the community center for practice, Madeline tried to forget that empty goodbye a few days ago. She'd known when she stepped into Jackson's life that he was a player. She'd known that the only reason he'd dragged her into his life was to help him with Jade.

She parked her car and walked up to the church. Beth Hightree met her at the steps.

"You look down tonight."

"I'm not down. I mean, not really. I'm just tired."

Beth nodded and Madeline thought she'd let it go. It would be good if she let it go. "I heard that Jackson brought Jade back home with him."

"He did."

"And she isn't his?" Beth walked with her through the old church sanctuary.

"Nope. But his name is on her birth certificate."

"Amazing. He's always had a big heart."

A big heart. Madeline nodded but she didn't want to talk about this anymore. She wanted to forget that Jackson had a big heart, that he cared about people. She wanted to remember him the way she used to think of him, as the man who knew how to charm, to smile and flirt but not remember a woman's name.

Beth continued to stare at her, obviously wanting an answer.

"He has a big heart." There, she'd agreed. Now let it go. Move on.

Beth laughed a little and reached to hug Madeline. "Oh, honey, you've fallen in love with that awful rogue."

"No, I haven't." Madeline reached for her shepherd's robe. "I helped him out when he needed help. End of story. Which is why I haven't talked to him since Saturday." She hadn't meant to add that.

"And you're going to let it go, just like that? Maybe he's been busy with Jade and hasn't had a spare minute to get in touch with you." Beth helped her pull down the rough, cotton gown. She handed Madeline the belt.

"Or maybe he's moved on. He's Jackson Cooper. Isn't that what he does?"

Beth took the belt from her hands and looped it twice around her waist, tying it at the side.

"In the past that's what he did. But I think he probably misses you as much as you miss him."

"This isn't me missing him. This is me being tired and ready for Christmas to be over."

"Right, you want Christmas to be over. You love Christmas."

"I do love Christmas." She loved the music, the decorations and most of all what the story meant to her life and to her faith. "I love it without the drama. And I don't mean the living nativity. I mean Jackson drama, Jade, and now my mother."

"She's contacted you again?"

Madeline pulled the shawl over her head to cover her hair.

"She wants to see me."

"You can't."

Madeline met her friend's concerned gaze. "I think I have to. I've thought about not seeing her. But I think I need closure. I need to face her. I have to do this or it will always control me."

"If you want, I'll go with you."

They hugged and Madeline nodded. "I'd love for you to go with me. I'm not running anymore, Beth. I'm not going to flee in fear that she'll find me. If I face her, I won't have to run again. I can stay here and let this be my home."

"I'm glad because I wouldn't want you to leave." Beth smiled a teasing smile. "And I think Jackson would miss you, too."

"I think what we need to do is get up there for this last practice."

Because she could only deal with one thing at a time. She would deal with her mother, with forgiving. Jackson was something she didn't want to think about. She didn't want to think about how he made her feel, or how much it hurt to think of that very quiet goodbye.

Jackson had needed a friend. Madeline smiled as they walked out of the dressing room. "You know, I'm just the person a guy calls when he needs a really big favor."

know, that I grew up with,
scue him."

. He said goodbye without
ll call you." Goodbye means

Chapter Sixteen

A few days before Christmas, Jackson walked through his house and it hit him that everything felt empty. Jade was staying with his grandmother for a few days. Madeline hadn't spoken to him since the day he dropped her off at her house.

The Christmas tree lights were unplugged. There were no gifts under his tree. It felt as much like Christmas as a hot day in July. Jackson Cooper, this is your life. This was reality.

He'd always liked it this way, empty, clean, quiet. Until it got filled up with Jade and Madeline, this life had been fine with him. They'd given him a brief glimpse into another world.

The doorbell chimed and the dog ran through the living room barking. Jackson yelled that he'd be there in a minute. When he opened the door his grandmother marched in, looking like a woman on a mission. With his grandmother, it was all about appearances. She had on her favorite hat, gloves and a dress coat over a pant-suit. And everyone new that Myrna Cooper loved her blue jeans. Suits were only for business and church. He grinned as she swooped in and he knew that he was her business.

"Where's Jade?" He looked behind her, looked at her car parked sideways in the drive.

"She's with Heather. They went Christmas shopping. Dear goodness, turn on some lights, this place looks and feels like a morgue. It's Christmas. Are you Scrooge?"

She walked ahead of him, flipping on lights, opening curtains. She plugged in the tree. "Nice tree. Buy some decorations next year."

"I like the homemade ones." Made by Madeline and Jade.

"Well, I never thought of you as the pitiful grandson."

"What does that mean?" He followed her into the kitchen where she turned on the coffeemaker. "I hear Travis brought a woman home with him. Harden's daughter?"

"Yeah, she's a looker."

Jackson laughed. "Gram, you're one of a kind."

She shrugged bony shoulders and turned to point a finger at him. Rings sparkled and bracelets clinked on her arms. "You're a mess."

"Could you explain what this visit is all about?"

"I'm here to save you."

"I think I've been saved. I'm even back in church. What more could you want?"

"I'm here to save you from your pitiful self. It was sweet of you to bring Jade back and give her a home, but you can't expect the rest of the family to raise her."

"I'm going to raise her."

"I know you are. You're going to find yourself a wife and you're going to raise that child the way she deserves, with you as a dad and with a decent woman as a mom."

"Gram, I'm not getting married."

"Oh, posh, stop that nonsense." She pulled a ring off her finger and handed it to him. "This ring was my grandmother's. I guess it's older than dirt, but it means something to me. It's about family, about history. You take this ring and you ask Madeline Patton to marry you."

He choked a little and put the ring back in her hand. "I don't know what you're up to, Gram, but I'm not asking Madeline to marry me."

"You hard-headed fool. That girl loves you and I'm pretty sure you love her, too."

He poured two cups of coffee. "I'm not in love. She helped me out. We're friends."

She frowned at him. "You're going to make me lose my witness if you don't stop acting so noble. Fine, you aren't sure. Date her for a while and then ask her to marry you."

"I'm not going to marry Madeline Patton."

Gram patted his cheek with a cool hand. He braced himself for it. Three little pats and then a good whack. He blinked and shook his head.

"Jackson, stop feeling sorry for yourself. Marry the girl."

She pushed the ring back into his hand. "And I don't want your coffee. It's always too strong and it gives me heartburn. I want you to invite Madeline to Christmas with the Coopers. She shouldn't be alone and you shouldn't want her to be alone."

"I'll think about it."

That pointy finger poked him in the gut. "You'd better do more than think about it. Now, I'm going home and I want you to get out of this house and go Christmas shopping. This place is a disgrace."

"Thanks, Gram, glad you approve."

She laughed as she walked through the house, grabbing her coat on her way out the door. "I love you, Jackson. You're my favorite."

"Gram, you say that to all of us."

She turned, smiling big. "I mean it, too."

That evening Jackson took Jade to see the living nativity. They took the tour of Bethlehem, met the innkeeper who turned Mary and Joseph away and then were led to the manger where the baby Jesus had been born. Through the crowds of people Jackson watched for the shepherdess who had touched his heart in a way he'd never expected.

Six months ago his brother Lucky had told him that someday he'd pay. He guessed this was what Lucky had meant. A woman had finally changed everything for him. She made him think about someone sitting next to him in those rocking chairs on his front porch.

He watched as she kneeled before Mary, Joseph and the baby Jesus. From Heather he'd learned that two days ago she had gone to Tulsa to see her mother. Beth had gone with her. He should have been the one to go with her.

Angels sang. The people in the crowd sang. The story of the birth of Jesus. The lighted star cast a bright light over the area, illuminating everything. Including the tears streaking down Madeline's cheeks.

"Are we going to talk to Madeline?" Jade had hold of his hand. Today he'd gone shopping and when Heather brought Jade to his house, the girl had screamed and raced around the house because of the gifts under the tree. His grandmother had been right. He'd played the part of Scrooge a little too well.

"Yes, we'll talk to her."

Jade led him through the crowd. Madeline had walked away from the other shepherds. She saw them heading her way and she froze.

"Madeline." Jackson didn't know what to say. He tried to remember a time in his life when a woman had left him speechless.

This had to be a first.

"Jackson." She smiled at Jade. "Hey, Jade, how are you?"

"I'm great. I have a ton of presents under the tree. And there are some for you, too."

"What?" Her gaze shot to Jackson's, asking questions.

The ball was in his court.

"We were wondering if you'd come to Christmas with us."

She looked at Jade and then at him. "Christmas?"

"With us," he repeated.

"Please." Jade grabbed her hand. "It won't be Christmas if you aren't with us."

Jackson reached for Jade. "She might have other plans. Do you have other plans?"

"No, I don't have other plans."

"Then you'll come." Jade didn't let her answer, but grabbed her in an exuberant hug. "Yeah!"

"Jade, she didn't say she would." Jackson shook his head. "I'm sorry."

"I'll go with you. What time?"

"We'll pick you up Christmas morning. Early. Maybe seven."

"I'll be ready."

Jackson took a step back because it would have been easy to reach out, to hold her. When it came to Madeline he was still fighting for self control.

Christmas with the Coopers. Madeline spent the next two days worrying, telling herself not to worry, being excited and then telling herself to stop. She had to get control of her emotions, shove them back in a box where they were safe.

Jackson had invited her for Jade's sake. Or maybe because the Coopers knew she'd be alone and they were just being polite. She didn't have to be alone on Christmas. Just over an hour away she had a mother living in Tulsa. Not that she was ready for serious family bonding with Marjorie. Not yet. They had talked. Marjorie had explained about growing up being shipped from relative to relative, getting pregnant and being on the streets until she'd formed a friendship with a group of people she thought would take care of her.

Madeline felt sorry for her mother. But the scars of the past were deep and healing would take time.

Beth Hightree had offered to let Madeline spend Christmas with her family, the Bradshaws. She didn't want to intrude on their family gathering, either. Yet she'd said yes to Jackson and Jade.

She'd even bought them gifts. Books for Jade because she loved to read. For Jackson, a coffee mug and gourmet coffee. She'd made candy to take for the rest of the Coopers. And there were a lot of them. Although a few would be missing. Reese had recently been sent to Afghanistan. Dylan had taken a load of bulls to California and on his way home he'd hit bad weather. He wouldn't be home for a day or two. That meant he'd miss Christmas with his family.

On Christmas morning she paced the living room, waiting for Jackson to show up. Hadn't he said he'd pick her up? What if he'd meant for her to drive herself? She paced back to the kitchen because she didn't want to look overly eager should he show up. If he hadn't changed his mind.

Her heart kept telling her to trust him, to give him a chance. If she didn't want to be judged for her past, Jackson shouldn't be judged for his. Not that he'd been the victim. She groaned at the wild storm of thoughts sweeping through her mind.

Deep breath, calm down. He hadn't invited her for any reason other than that Jade probably wanted her there. Another deep breath. That made perfect sense. Jade had missed her.

The doorbell rang and the puppy, cast-free now, ran in circles, barking and jumping. Madeline slowed her pace and walked calmly to the door. She opened it and a bouquet of flowers and balloons attacked.

"Oops, sorry." Jackson moved the bouquet and smiled.

Her heart did a triple back flip. He grinned and pushed his hat back a little.

"What's this?"

He handed her the vase. "Merry Christmas."

"Thank you." She tried to smell the white roses and red carnations but balloon strings were everywhere. "These probably don't mess on the floor or chew up slippers."

"Not that I've heard of, but if they do, let me know." He followed her inside and she carried the vase of flowers to the kitchen table.

When Madeline turned, he was standing right behind her. She stepped back and looked up, afraid,

nt things at once. Afraid of
ay or wouldn't say.
ached for her purse.

ee."

istead of walking away, he
top her. "You forgot to read

he note and opened it. He
me."

nbled. Her hands trembled.
that felt like trembling. Or

ou go steady with a cowboy
oly is, in love with you?"
ne?"

with you I can't see straight."
Then he leaned, still holding
sweetly, stealing her heart,
ver imagined. In his arms she
oved.

, she rested her head on his
. I was just so afraid."

n looked up. "Afraid that
verything in my past, I just

You're strong, brave and beau-
hat is too much. It floors me
here with a renegade like me."
say." She didn't know what
it losing it right there, stand-

"Madeline, you have to go into this knowing that I can't have children. I'll adopt as many as you want to fill that old farmhouse with. But that's something I've been running from for a long time."

"We have Jade."

"We." He hugged her tight. "I love it when we're a 'we.'"

Jackson reached into his pocket, laughing a little at the surprised look on Madeline's face. "I know we just started going steady—" he glanced at his watch "—two minutes ago, so this probably seems like the shortest courtship in the world, but I have another question I'd like to ask, and if I don't do this right, my grandmother is going to flog me good."

"Okay."

"Now bear with me, I'm not as young as I used to be and you might have to help me get up."

She laughed. He shot her a look, trying to appear offended that she'd laugh at him.

"Jackson, please don't."

"Are you really going to laugh at a man who is trying to propose the way his Gram expects him to propose, the way a gentleman proposes?"

She laughed until tears sprang from her eyes. Jackson reached for a napkin on the kitchen table and handed it to her.

"Now let's start over. And please, no laughing. I got a two-hour lesson on courting and proposals last night." He winked and Madeline turned pink. "I think Gram might have mentioned that the courting part of the process should last at least six months and then the proposal. But I've always been a renegade when it comes to love. I'm afraid if I don't get this ring on your finger, you'll chicken out or realize I'm not much of a catch."

"Jackson, I love you. But really, I do think we should, um, date? For a few months at least."

"Stop talking, you're throwing me off my groove. You know, I used to have a groove until you came along and completely threw me for a loop." He took off his hat and tossed it on the table. With her hand in his he dropped to one knee and fished the ring out of his pocket again.

"Please, stop." Tears poured down her cheeks. Jackson stopped.

"Are you going to say no?" He didn't know how long he could stay on one knee. He wasn't many weeks this side of being tossed into a wall.

She shook her head. "I'm not going to say no, but it's so much and it's Christmas and…"

He grinned big and she smiled. "And you love me because I'm crazy and nothing like any other man you've ever met. Madeline, you need a man like me, someone strong and stubborn. I'm not going to let you go. I'm not going to hurt you."

The ring in his hand, more than a hundred years old, sparkled and the metal heated in his hand. He slid it on her finger. "My great-grandfather gave this ring to his wife. When my grandmother got married, they gave it to her to wear. She wanted you to have it because she wanted you to know that when you marry me, you're a Cooper. We marry for life and we hold on to each other through life's storms."

"Did your grandmother tell you to say all of that?"

He grinned and shook his head, but then he nodded.

"Some of it."

Madeline fell to her knees in front of him. He forgot

about his aching knees when she cupped his cheeks in her sweet hands and moved close, touching her lips to his.

He forgot about everything but Madeline and how it felt to hold her in his arms. He'd spent a lifetime thinking he'd never get caught, only to find out that it wasn't about getting caught, it was about falling. And falling.

With Madeline, he thought he'd be falling in love with her for the rest of their lives. He told her that and she wrapped her arms around his neck and buried her face in his shoulder.

"Madeline, will you marry me?"

She nodded. "I will."

"Then you'd better help me up and we'd better get to the house before they send out a search party."

She stood, reaching for his hands and pulling him to his feet.

"Where's Jade?" Madeline's eyes watered and her nose was pink.

"I'm right here."

They turned and Jade was standing in the door of the kitchen with Angel the puppy. "I think that was about the sappiest proposal ever."

Madeline reached for his hand and held it tight. "I think it was the sweetest proposal ever."

Jade ran forward and hugged them both. "The best part is that I'm going to have a family. Merry Christmas!"

"Merry Christmas, Jade." Jackson hugged the girl who was his. It didn't matter what the DNA test said—in his heart, she was his daughter. They were a family, and he'd never had a better Christmas or been more blessed in his life.

Brenda K

about his aching knees a bao
her sweet hands and moved a
his.

He freed about everythin
fair to hold her in his arms. H
ing he'd never get caught, onl
about getting caught; it was a

With Madeline, he foun
with her for the rest
she wrapped her arm
face in his shoulder.

"Madame, will you marr

She nodded. "I will."

"Then you'd better help

logue

w of the Sunday school class-
dress for the wedding and she
you have to see this."

w and shook her head. "No,
rprise."

e past Beth but several pairs
kept her from getting a look

ven think about it." Angie
ckson went to a lot of trouble
uin it for him."

yes but she giggled. "You re-
ht?"

ouldn't walk right for a week.
keep the ring until after you'd

need to see what's out there.
line looked around the room,
lling to spill the secret. Her

bridesmaids, Jenna, Beth, Heather and Jade, all shook their heads.

The only other person in the room shook her head, too. Madeline's mother, Marjorie, was a thin, tiny woman. She no longer looked beaten down by life. Her eyes had a spark that hadn't been there months ago when they'd met in Tulsa. They were getting to know each other again.

Madeline had a family. She smiled at Jade, remembering a teenager who had defied everyone to get that exact same thing for herself.

Jade twirled in her pale yellow dress. "I love this dress."

"Don't get it dirty," Madeline warned. "Or trip over the hem."

"I won't." Jade weaved, dizzy from turning in circles. "I wish I could go to Hawaii with you."

"Sorry, this is a honeymoon for two. When we get home we'll take you to Florida, remember?"

"I remember." Jade's smile brightened. "And I get to stay with Grandma Angie while you're gone."

"Yes, you do." Madeline looked in the mirror at her simple, white dress. Straight lines, no beading or lace. She'd never thought about weddings or what she would wear. She'd never dreamed of honeymoons or even the man who would change her life.

And yet he had existed anyway. All of those years of closing herself off, afraid to feel, afraid of being hurt again, and God already had the perfect man for her.

Jackson Cooper. She smiled at her reflection in the mirror. In a million years she wouldn't have thought he would be the one. It wasn't that long ago that she'd avoided looking him in the eye when he helped pick up her spilled groceries.

s *Holiday Blessing*

before God, in the presence
ould become her husband.

Madeline Cooper. Maddie
yes as love and contentment
ened them, Beth stood behind

Madeline. He took all of your
curity upon Himself and gave
w hope."

kson's sister Sophia, self-ap-
inator, smiled and motioned

v on the road."

ie." Heather patted her sister
d out of the room.

romance."

Angie Cooper shook her head
daughter's cheek. "Romance

s dad, stood at the entrance to
eady to walk Madeline down
andsome in his Western-cut
gaze slid past him to the front
her hand on his arm and they
bridesmaids walking in front

ly for the man at the front of
per, the man she would spend
inutes later he slipped a wed-
, sliding it against the ring his
ded. They said "I do" and he
g her as if he would never let
her down the aisle and out the

To her surprise a white open carriage was parked in front of the church. Adorned with white roses, it was pulled by four white horses. A man in white livery stood next to the door of the carriage, holding it open for them.

"Surprise." Jackson leaned and kissed her cheek.

"It's a wonderful surprise."

"Throw the bouquet," someone shouted.

Madeline turned her back to the crowd and tossed the yellow daisies and white roses. The bouquet landed right in Sophia Cooper's hands.

* * * * *

ek! I've gotten very attached
d to the Cooper family. With
ere will be plenty to keep us
Most importantly there will
1 was Harlequin's YEAR OF
will provide many more cow-
And of course wonderful hero-
those cowboys to fall in love.
en around Dawson for a while
g that he be the first hero in
atched his friends and neigh-
getting married. He warned
el Waters would get under his
ckson Cooper, resident ladies'
nune to love.

ckson had his ideas about his
: set of plans. So make a cup
some Christmas music and
awson, Oklahoma, at Christ-

Questions for Discussion

1. Madeline Patton finds herself in a situation she wants to walk away from. Instead she puts herself and her heart on the line by agreeing to allow Jade Baker to stay in her home. Why would she make that decision?

2. Jackson Cooper asks Madeline to let Jade stay with her. He has several reasons. What are they? Do you agree with the choices he made?

3. Jackson is torn when he looks up Madeline on the internet. Like so many of us, he was curious. But learning her story put him in a situation where he had more knowledge than perhaps he had wanted. How does this information change his relationship with her?

4. Jackson has a certain reputation, but as we get to know him we see that being a "ladies' man" is just one facet of his personality and life. Who is the real Jackson Cooper?

5. Madeline receives a card from her mother that she doesn't immediately open. Why doesn't she want to face her mother's words? What would you have done?

6. Why has Madeline been in the habit of moving? Why is it important for her to stay in Dawson?

7. Jackson goes back to church. Did he have a real reason for walking away from his faith?

8. Why do you think Madeline sleeps with the lights on? She has faith but still struggles with fear. How does Jackson help her through these fears? How does she help herself?

9. Madeline is hurt by what she sees as Jackson's rejection. How does this draw her out of her shell?

10. Why is Jackson being so careful in his relationship with Madeline?

11. Jackson remembers the chorus of his grandmother's favorite hymn. The lines in the chorus are "No turning back, no turning back." What do the words mean to Jackson in his personal growth? In his relationship?

12. Jackson knew from the beginning that Jade couldn't be his child and yet he allowed her to stay. Why do you think he allowed her to stay?

13. Madeline has forgiven her mother but there is still pain. Is it realistic to think she should give in and develop a relationship with her mother or is caution the best way to handle this relationship?

14. Jackson and Madeline fall in love rather quickly and both realize that they need more time to get to know one another. Love is based on more than immediate attraction. What is the basis for their relationship, beyond those first feelings of chemistry?

INSPIRATIONAL

Wholesome romances that touch the heart and soul.

Love Inspired

COMING NEXT MONTH
AVAILABLE DECEMBER 27, 2011

SEASIDE REUNION
Starfish Bay
Irene Hannon

LONGING FOR HOME
Mirror Lake
Kathryn Springer

DADDY'S LITTLE MATCHMAKERS
Second Time Around
Kathleen Y'Barbo

THE DOCTOR'S SECRET SON
Email Order Brides
Deb Kastner

MONTANA MATCH
Merrillee Whren

SMALL-TOWN SWEETHEARTS
Jean C. Gordon

Look for these and other Love Inspired books wherever books are sold, including most bookstores, supermarkets, discount stores and drug stores.   LICNM1211

Love Inspired

After surviving a devastating tragedy, combat reporter Nate Garrison returns home to Starfish Bay. But his reunion with lovely Lindsey Collier is nothing like he's dreamed. Lindsey is now a sad-eyed widow who avoids loss and love. Knowing he's been given a second chance, Nate sets out to show her faith's true healing power.

Seaside Reunion
by Irene Hannon

ZGERALD BAY *series*
e, law enforcement siblings
ly when one of their own
of murder.

eview of the first book,
ACY by Shirlee McCoy.

erald stepped into his father's
clan had gathered, and he was
em. He had a foolproof excuse.
 father had raised him. It was
 be.

ning room. With his boisterous
 never be empty.

 when he felt that something

his thoughts, his radio crackled

tion on our hands. A body has
se."

he caller believes the deceased

glas's brother Charles spoke.
 twin toddlers, he employed

utes." He jogged back outside

 Street and out onto the rural
Two police cars followed. His
glas was sure of it. Together,

they'd piece together what had happened.

The lighthouse loomed in the distance, growing closer with every passing mile. A beat-up station wagon sat in the driveway.

Douglas got out and made his way along the path to the cliff.

Up ahead, a woman stood near the edge.

Meredith O'Leary.

There was no mistaking her strawberry-blond hair, her feminine curves, or the way his stomach clenched, his senses springing to life when he saw her.

"Merry!"

"Captain Fitzgerald! Olivia is…"

"Stay here. I'll take a look."

He approached the cliff's edge. Even from a distance, Douglas recognized the small frame.

His father stepped up beside him. "It's her."

"I'm afraid so."

"We need to be the first to examine the body. If she fell, fine. If she didn't, we need to know what happened."

If she fell.

The words seemed to hang in the air, the other possibilities hovering with them.

*Can Merry work together with Douglas to find justice for
Olivia…without giving up her own deadly secrets?
To find out, pick up
THE LAWMAN'S LEGACY by Shirlee McCoy,
on sale January 10, 2012.*

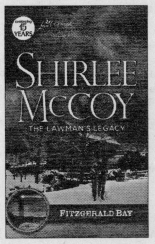